The
Burnt Roses

Jon Ferguson

Huge Jam Publishing
Gravenhurst, England, 2023

ISBN: 978-1911249986

Please note that this novel is set in the 1970s and the decades preceding it. Several characters respond to events, in dialogue and in action, that we know to be unacceptable today. That they do so is part of their own tragedies and as such integral to the narrative.

The author's own inclusive philosophy is made clear in his non-fiction:

"All the anger the old man saw flowing from the TV saddened him. He wondered why all human beings still hadn't realized that every human being had a story to tell, and that all human beings were the most important creatures in the world, at least for themselves. He wondered why something so obvious was so difficult for people to understand... why respecting the existence of all creatures was so difficult."

(The Old Man and the Stone, Jon Ferguson, ISBN: 978-1-916604-00-1)

Ash on an old man's sleeve
Is all the ash the burnt roses leave.
Dust in the air suspended
Marks the place where the story ended.
Dust inbreathed was a house—
The wall, the wainscot and the mouse.
The death of hope and despair,
This is the death of air.

T. S. Eliot
Little Gidding

I

"Our Father in Heaven we're thankful that we could all be here today and sit around this table and have Thanksgiving and especially we're thankful that Aunt Rilda and Aunt Martha could come and for the popcorn that Aunt Rilda always brings. Bless the food on this table that it will nourish and strengthen our bodies and do us the good we need and we're grateful for Mommy who cooks the meals and for Daddy who makes the money and for Wayne and Amber and bless Grandma and Grandpa and the people in China…and we thank Thee for the head over our…for the roof of our heads and for everything…and we say these things in the name of Jesus Christ amen."

"Amen."

"Hey Aaron, who told you to say that stuff about China?"

"Mom can I have all white meat and a lot of dressing, but leave off those orange potatoes?"

"Yes dear."

"Honey it was one helluva game. You should have seen ol' Max McGee waltz through the Lion secondary. He should have been wearing a tux."

"Joan, light on the gravy."

"Any dark meat Rilda?"

"Oh Joan, give me a sliver."

"Martha?"

"All or nothing…"

"Wayne dear, could you get me an extra plate in the kitchen for this skin here."

"Who'd you say won Elroy?"

"Packers – Starr to McGee down and out, Hornung on the sweep, Taylor up the middle. They might as well put the sons a bitches…"

"Honey!"

"Hey Dad can you pass the corn?"

"Here ya go."

"That was a nice prayer Aaron and you keep it up."

"Joan your dressing smells divine."

"Thank you Rilda."

"Here Mom. Dad who'd you say won?"

"Green Bay, thirty-five to… Martha… Martha! Martha! What the hell do you think…"

Aunt Martha had the carving knife aimed at a purple flower in the middle of her paisley dress.

"Stay right where you are all of you. This is my business," she said rising. She back-pedalled to the door to the back patio, opened it with her left hand, wedged her way out, and stumbled into the ping-pong table. She scuttled to the wooden gate and headed resolutely into the green autumn hills of Orinda.

Immolation really was on Martha's mind, but as she climbed the hill behind the Elroy house she was yet unsure as to what she would sacrifice herself for. That morning as she bathed she had considered writing a note. While scrubbing under her arms she thought she would do it for the Native American. A few years before, she had filled a plastic bag with worn pullovers for the Navajo in southern Utah. But that was in 1970 and it was difficult to thrust a knife into your gut for people who might not be cold anymore. As she washed between her toes she imagined writing, "I give myself not to death but to the Negroes in Washington D.C and all territories that wrapped brothers and sisters in the cold iron knuckles of slavery." But the farthest she'd been east was Winnemucka, Nevada to play silver dollar slot machines on her honeymoon. Lathering and soaking the rest of her body she considered, at least briefly, killing herself for: those who died in the Titanic catastrophe, worms threaded on fish hooks, worms crushed on sidewalks in the rain, victims of the two world wars, victims of all wars going back to the Battle of Hastings, wilted flowers, hooked fish, all furry animals caught in traps, cows that mistakenly wandered into traps, insects, Abraham Lincoln, pioneers, shooting stars, Jesus, the French actress Arletty (still living at the time), pregnant women, polio victims, Africa, the blind, the ordinary, the turkey, God, Lucille Ball (also living), Ponce de Leon, nonvenomous snakes, cowards, klepto-maniacs, oranges, leathery corpses under avalanches, hypochondriacs, and butterflies.

When Elroy pushed the screen door and followed Martha into the hills, he had the impression he was running an end-around. He faked left and scooted by the incinerator. He slipped but regained his footing when he passed the Healy's peach tree. As he headed upfield he could hear his son Wayne in heavy pursuit. Then, like spotting pay dirt, he saw his sister. She was lugging herself upward through the grass holding the knife as if it were a wand. Like most widows she was overweight and the climb was starting to get to her. She stopped and stood beneath an oak tree near Bob Seaman's house. The tree was a wonder of symmetry that Elroy had admired when returning an oil can or a hedge trimmer to Seaman. Now he approached his sister and put forth his hand.

"Give me the knife Martha," he whispered.

Being right-handed she held the knife to Elroy's left. She spread her arms to full length and perpendicular to the trunk of the tree. As she did this she wondered why she extended her left arm as well as the right. The right she understood – she wanted to take advantage of a full thrust. But the left?

Wayne stopped some twenty yards behind his father. It had rained, the hill was muddy and the grass around him was the colour of mint. Wayne looked skyward beseeching and tried to pull down some form of help from behind the heavy grey roof of the coastal clouds.

"Martha, drop it," Elroy said. He wanted to follow this up with a reason but he couldn't think of one. He was trying to prevent his sister's suicide because doing otherwise had never occurred to him. He was now close enough to tackle her. He planted his left foot, but the ground was slippery. He was Ray Nietzsche without cleats on. Could he make the tackle in JC Penney wingtips? Martha mumbled something (her final reason) that Elroy took to be a quarterback audible. Her right elbow snapped. Elroy dove and rammed his shoulder into her left hip. This spun her and the knife slammed into the oak tree. Martha's hand slid across the blade severing all the tendons in her fingers. She fainted in Elroy's grasp. Wayne ran up to the Seaman's and Bob Seaman left his own Thanksgiving feast to help carry Martha down the hill. A half hour later she was lifted into an ambulance and taken to Kaiser Hospital in Walnut Creek.

Elroy, unlike his sister, had never wished to die. Actually, he never thought about it. For Martha, living and not living were an obsession. Where she saw life there was death. A birth was a funeral. But Elroy was the kind of person who, needing a new shirt, could walk into a shop, see a beige striped button-down on sale near the door for a rock bottom price and buy it without even the slightest glance at the racks of Hathaways, Gants, or Evan-Picones. In restaurants he never looked at menus but ordered what looked good on the nearest tables. He loved the Packers, not because he had ever set foot in Green Bay but because his house in Orinda was on Lombardy Lane and Lombardi was the coach. The y and the i presented no contradiction.

He was a Mormon because his mother had been one. Though prohibited by the religion, he drank rivers of beer because the bubbles, the foam, and the light syrupy consistency were, as he said, the waters in which angels swam. His large aquiline nose was never the source of comparative anxiety.

Even love was without paradox, contradiction, and pain. Elroy chose his wife as he would have picked the beige shirt. He was twenty-four and late for an appointment to replace a filling in a molar in the upper right quadrant of his jaw. He ran into a building he thought was his dentist's. He found himself in a typing class of a secretarial school. Thirty young women looked up from their machines at a panting Elroy. Second from the right on the first row sat Joan Hatch. She was the only thing in the room Elroy saw. Her cheeks were flushed, her eyes bright blue, her ankles thin and comely. Elroy left the room, waited until class dismissed and married Joan five weeks later without another thought for the hole in his tooth, the twenty-nine other secretaries, or – for that matter – the millions of other adult women puttering about the globe.

When they married, Elroy was in the FBI. The war was on and he had been assigned to the pursuit of draft dodgers. He spent numerous hot summer nights trying to consummate the marriage. Joan Hatch Elroy was from Orem, Utah. Having been told for twenty years that the links of the steel chain of sin were murder, adultery, fornication, masturbation, and heavy petting, it was difficult for her to allow a wedding ceremony to immediately thaw the frozen apparatus of the flesh.

Summer had failed to melt the ice. But, when autumn came, the following happened:

Elroy had been chasing a man who got on a train for New York. Elroy followed and made his arrest more quickly than expected in a donut shop not far from the Edison Hotel. Hence, Elroy was a married twenty-four-year-old male virgin with some free time on his hands in the most feculent and fecund city in the world. He was a firecracker in a blazing forest.

He went to Times Square and was accosted by a young woman in a lime green dress and attractive elevated shoes. She was pleasant, not pushy, and invited him for a cup of coffee. They sat across from each other in a booth in a Hot Shoppe and ordered their coffee. The woman extended her leg under the formica table and pushed it against Elroy's tibia. Elroy had always thought that brain could act on body and vice versa, but now the two, brain and body, were like a raging bonfire. Her calf ambled to his knee and that was enough for Elroy. Between his legs his flower burst, his pants were watered, and he saved himself twenty dollars and probably his marriage.

The young lady excused herself leaving a dime on the table. She tossed Elroy a "maybe some other time", seeming to genuinely like him, then disappeared into the forest. Elroy sat in the booth and waited for his trousers to dry.

His thoughts were now on his wife. He loved her. It was she he wanted naked before him. It was with her he wanted to break his silence and let his engines roar. She was his Eve. He her Adam. He assured himself with these ideas until he was free to stand up. He went to a telephone box and called Joan long distance. She said she'd be on the next train and Elroy went to the Edison and booked a room.

What happened to Joan Elroy on the train from Baltimore to New York would have put other women on a doctor's couch. But she believed in the love and grace of God and not in the kingdom of psychiatry. The world was not complicated. It had been lovely in Orem, it was lovely in Baltimore, and it would be lovely when they moved to California. For her life was only problematical in recipe books, on tax forms, and below the belly button. When she saw a dead cat on the highway, she knew it was already in heaven.

It was Thursday afternoon. She boarded the train at 16:36. It wasn't overcrowded. She took a window seat across the aisle from a pleasant looking man in a bowler hat and a raincoat. It was cloudy but not raining. The landscape as they left the city reminded Joan of Utah. There were white houses with fences, horses here and there, and she watched the green of the fields slowly mix with the grey sky until all was darkness. She looked across the aisle and the man in the bowler seemed to be sleeping. He roused as they pulled into Philadelphia, then lifted his raincoat and exposed himself as the train chugged out of the city of brotherly love.

It took Joan several seconds to make sense out of what the man was doing. The comfortable monotony of trains puts us in strange states. His member was not fully inflated. Joan was neither disgusted nor shocked for the simple reason that what she was staring at reminded her of a planarian. To say "reminded" is not exact. She had seen a photograph of this *Tricladida* order flatworm four years before in her college biology textbook. She was now looking at the same image. Her fixed glance blocked out the man, the seats, and the windows of the train. She was sitting motionless in a well-lit library looking at a picture of a broad worm with a tri-branched digestive cavity.

It must be understood that for Joan Hatch biology had been a course in empathy and love; all living things were God's creations and God was good. Streptococci were cute under the microscope and were part of a divine plan. Mud eels (*Siren lacertian*) were to be loved like dogs and cats. Even efts (*Diemictylus viridenscens*) somehow touched the highest reaches of heaven. Now Joan was staring at an innocent empyrean planarian. It was another part of God's goods.

When she got to New York her cosmology now held the male sex gland to be as noble as the flatworm.

Elroy met here at Grand Central, then took her to the Edison where they had the time of their lives.

*

Sewing tendons together takes time so the doctors in Walnut Creek put Martha out. The anaesthetist placed a small mask over her nose and mouth and pumped in the ether. Martha counted to three and was as good as dead for the next nine hours.

When she came to, her hand and forearm were in a cast and she was in a metal bed next to a large woman who had lost her covers, was snoring, and had plaster of Paris from thigh to ankle on both legs. Had Martha not been drugged she would have been annoyed. Instead she climbed out of bed, rummaged through the woman's handbag, found a pen, and with her left hand scribbled, "Best of Luck Your Friend Martha", around the woman's kneecaps. Then she fell back to sleep for three more hours. This time she dreamt.

She was in a meadow filled with dragonflies. The biggest dragonflies were the Elroy twins. Aaron and Amber, whose wings were the length of oars. She was reading a book about silk painting but she had no arms and was unable to turn the pages. The twins did this for her. When she finished the book she cried, "Let there be paint!", and the wings of all the dragonflies were instantly covered with colourful flower designs like those in late Matisse cut-outs. (That Martha didn't know of Matisse makes her dream remarkable.) Then all the dragonflies surrounded her, clamped their feet to her body, and lifted her to heaven where, armless, she signed autographs for all the Apostles.

*

When she woke up the second time she was looking at her brother and Ramon Navarro. Surprised to have arms, she snatched the pen off her bed table and intending to prolong the autograph session said, "For you, Navarro, I'll sign, but you, Elroy, get the hell out of here."

Martha had a strange habit which was here at work. She was often unable to look at people's entire faces. She would, for example, see a nose on a bus – a nose that looked exactly like the nose of someone she knew. Her imagination would then amplify the nose and she would be sure she was looking at an acquaintance.

The nose on the bus would be her neighbour's, Helen Ruffenacht's nose. "Have you trimmed the roses?" she might say, and the stranger would move to another seat. "Are your kidney stones still bothering you?" and Martha's pardon would be begged.

The doctor standing over her had Ramon Navarro's eyes. His name was Ernest Winquist but Martha, now aware no one in the room wanted her signature, insisted on calling him Mr. Navarro.

"I'm thirsty, Mr. Navarro," she said.

"I'm Dr. Winquist, but I'm sure the nurse can get you something. How is your hand feeling?"

"Can't feel a thing, Mr. Navarro. Elroy, I thought I told you to get the hell out?"

"Martha, his name is Winquist," Elroy said exchanging glances with the doctor. "I'm here to take you home. The doctor says you don't need to stay for observation."

"I haven't been home for sixty years and you're damned not the one who's going to take me there!" Dr. Winquist put a calm hand on Martha's shoulder. "Now maybe Mr. Navarro here could take me home…"

"I'll call the nurse," the surgeon said politely excusing himself.

Martha changed into her bloodstained paisley dress. In the corridor they met a nurse with a glass of orange juice. "Drink it yourself, honey," Martha said and they stepped into the parking lot.

Elroy's car was an old pink Cadillac. Aunt Rilda told him it was the colour of the marble columns of the Grand Trianon in Versailles. Above each taillight was a small fin like that of a grayling and it could seat seven comfortably.

Martha lived in Concord six miles away. They got on highway 680 and drove out of Walnut Creek. The hills around them were soft and tremulous and reminded Elroy of the female side of nature. They bore peaches, pears, apples, and plums with equal facility, mostly in backyards. In summer the hills were a mass of straw except for sundry black rectangles where fire had scarred them. Now, in November, they were emerald. They stretched from Berkeley through Orinda, on to Pleasant Hill and Concord, and then flattened out where the Central Valley began.

Martha lived on Willow Path Road in what today would be called a "dive" and was then known as a "shack". Her biggest room was the kitchen. In one corner sat a bulbous Westinghouse refrigerator covered with postcards from friends, Austria and Switzerland ("royal palaces, sapient citizens", she said) that she had bought at the flea market on a Saturday morning at the Yo-Ho Drive-In Theater. Otherwise there was a sink, a grey cupboard, and an old wooden table above which hung a portrait entitled *La Duchesse de Chartres en Hébé*. The Duchess was wearing a low-cut dress and had flowers in her hair. In her right hand she held a watering jug. Her left hand wasn't painted. The small print under the reproduction read, *Jean-Marc Nattier, Né à Paris (1685-1766). Devenu en 1740 peintre attitré de la Cour, il est l'auteur des nombreux portraits, presque tous féminins.* There was a bit too much space between the Duchess's eyes, but her tiny mouth and chin made up for it and she could be called beautiful.

Martha couldn't read French (who in Concord could?) but she could say it. "Hey, Elroy, get a look at my new picture. Got it at the flea market. It's *lah dutchess dee chart-ress en heebee.* Nice, ehh?"

"Very nice, Martha," her brother said.

"It's very modern don't you think?" said Martha. Elroy looked at the caption.

"It says seventeen-something," he said.

"I know. In seventeen-something it was very modern and I still think of it that way. If you only think what exists today is modern, nothing's modern because today is always yesterday before you know it. But if you think of things the day they were made then everything's modern. If you really think about it – Elroy – everything's either really modern or really old. This half and half stuff is a crock of crap."

"Maybe you've got something there," Elroy said.

"Can I get you anything before I go?"

"No. You've been a wonderful help," said Martha. She wasn't being sarcastic. She meant it. She always meant everything.

"Goodbye, Elroy."

Martha was not poor. She lived in a shack to save money. Her husband died in Camp Pendleton while learning the art of war. His name had been Ray Hiller. He was shooting his M-1 at a dummy head that was sticking out of the top of a tank. A bullet, possibly his own, ricocheted off the tank and went through his neck. In the hospital a note was found in his boot. It is the last thing known about him. It read: "The Letter M that I fire began around 1000 B.C. when the Phoenicians and other Semites of Syria and Palestine started to use a graphic sign representing the consonant m. They named the sign mem, meaning water. After 900 B.C. the Greeks borrowed the sign from the Phoenicians in modified form, altering its name to mu. They later reversed its orientation and gradually eliminated its tail, giving it a symmetrical form. The Greek forms passed unchanged via Etruscans to the Romans; they developed the Monumental Capital that is the basis of our modern capital printed and written. The written Roman forms developed into the late Roman and medieval Uncial and Cursive, which are the basis of our modern small letter, printed and written, m as in mulberry mound modesto munch middle marry martha. R.H."

For her husband's death Martha was given a medal of the Order of the Purple Heart and thirty thousand dollars in life insurance. She put all this (medal and cash) in the Bank of America and hasn't touched it since. She says she's saving for a trip, "to see if the world is bigger or smaller than I think it is and to see if there's some place I like better than myself."

*

Why was Elroy a virgin until the night with Joan in the Edison Hotel?

We know the reasons for the early difficulties with his wife, but why, prior to her, had he never slept with a woman?

Elroy spent the first ten years of life in the sainted town of Pocatello in southern Idaho. The Mormons, Presbyterians, Methodists, Baptists and Adventists had arrived. The automobile and psychiatry were not far behind. Elroy lived with Martha and their parents above the family drugstore on Main Street. At any given moment from sunup to sundown Elroy could look out his bedroom window and see at least one servant of the Lord pushing his or her boots along the sidewalk in the direction of some good deed. There was Brother Perkins taking a bouquet of daisies to the widow Smythe. Sister Wignal was carrying a pot of stew to Brother Marsing who at eighty couldn't walk, but from the back of the chapel in his wheelchair could hit every note of "The Spirit of God Like a Fire Is Burning". Or there, across the street, was young Deacon Whitimore collecting tithes from Brother Hutchinson, Pocatello's only barber. He could see Elder Blosil, a hammer dangling from his burlap jeans, on his way to nail together the Campbell's dilapidated barn. And there, crossing in front of Hansen's General Store, little Jamie Fowler in his black hat was mouthing verses from Isaiah and Ezekiel. Or Elroy might catch sight of Bishop Merriner McKinnon, smile on his face, toting a basket of eggs for the pancakes at the church bazaar.

Of course Pocatello had its underside. Of course Brother Perkin's handful of daisies sprung from his crotch. Of course Elder Blosil wielded his shiny hammer to attract the eyes of Sharon, the pretty Campbell girl. Naturally Sister Wignal's pot of stew smelled of hope for a pocketful of old Marsing's legacy. We needn't even mention what shook the walls and rattled the dishes a mile out of town on the

Ledbedder farm.

What is of interest here is what young Elroy saw as the world marched beneath his window. It was holy. It was the reflection of the Saviour Himself, with one exception. The aberration was his own father. His mother told him so.

Sarah Elroy wore pins in her hair and often removed the most pointed one to plant in her husband's arse as he stood behind the counter in his drugstore. She hated the place. It smelled of mercurochrome and sulphur and potassium nitrate.

One morning in mid-March Sarah grabbed her son and tromped downstairs. She was like a one-woman vice squad dropping in on Hades. And she needed a witness. "Materialism, godless materialism!" she shouted. "There's not an ounce of righteousness in this hellhole! The place smells like the devil's underwear! You don't save souls with sulphur dioxide and I guarantee your sorry soul that Jesus never gave out a pill in his life! The Lord works in miracles, not molecules, and I should have known better than to marry a rancid compound like you!"

Sarah ended her tirade by heaving a bottle marked SO_2NH_2 at the soda fountain. She stomped her heels, did an about-face, and dragged her son out the door and in the direction of Bishop McKinnon's house.

Elroy never saw his father again. The man packed

his things that same morning and made his way into Montana where he eventually opened another drugstore in Great Falls at the corner of South Main and Third Street. He sold sodas and sulphur until he died of a heart attack at the age of sixty-eight in the arms of a woman he called, "My Tender Grizzly…"

And Elroy's virginity?

Mother and son went to the McKinnon's. Bishop McKinnon was feeding corn nuggets to the chickens. "Greetings Sister Elroy and greetings little Elroy," he said.

"Bishop!" Sarah said with lips drawn, "Where does your wife go on Monday mornings?"

"To do Relief Society work."

"No she doesn't. She takes her quilt and meets my husband at Harlow's pond."

"Sister Sarah…"

"Brother William… If the Lord lives we share our beds with fornicators and defecators!"

"Have mercy," the Bishop whispered skyward.

"Have mercy," Sarah repeated as she clutched her son's hand and led him out of the chicken coop.

Mother and son walked back through town, past the white Adventist church, past the white Methodist church, past Hansen's General Store, and past the white Mormon chapel to the big birch tree between Wright's Livery and the Baptist Hall.

Sarah Elroy sat her boy down and gave him a lavish sermon touching the sacred and the profane, the ugly and the beautiful, the rich and the poor, the soiled and the clean, the debased and the noble, and his father and the good Brother Perkins. Under the shimmering leaves of the birch, she made her son swear to chastity, marriage, and fidelity in that order.

Come June, Sarah and her two children moved to Portland. Here she made her son repeat his vows on a bed of pine needles in a rainstorm.

When a year later they migrated south to Sacramento, Elroy said "yes" "yes" "yes" on the steps of the Capital.

By the time they got to Oakland, Elroy was fourteen and had an uncontrollable appetite for chilidogs. Here Sarah put him face to face with a menu at the Doggie Diner on MacArthur Avenue. For the last time Elroy swore to his mother's version of goodness and then ate to his heart's content.

The only real occasion where Elroy could have cheated on his mother was with the woman in the lime green dress. But under the table in the Hot Shoppe one of Nature's self-regulatory mechanisms took hold and the geyser went off before Elroy could get anybody wet.

Wayne Elroy was conceived on the eighth floor of the Edison Hotel. If, as some believe, our lives and characters are not determined by chromosomes or galaxies or our social surroundings, but rather by the joy and intensity (or lack of) of the two participants at the moment of our making, then Wayne Elroy ought to have been the happiest person alive.

By the time his wife got off the train in New York, Elroy had stored up enough vigour and passion to satisfy half the females in Manhattan. Joan got it all. And she – miraculously raised by the planarian-penis from the latter-day-sainted puritanical quagmire of which the town of Orem was but a puddle – was the perfect partner.

Room 818 was fifteen feet by twelve with walls, ceiling and bedspread a uniform faded turquoise. The carpet under their feet looked like a Mesozoic beach littered with ammonites. Elroy threw his wife into the furrow in the centre of the bed and through the night they, man and woman, were a two-headed octopus riding the surface of a great prehistoric sea. New life was bred. In this case their first son.

Martha was conceived in another corner of the rainbow. In June of 1913 Samuel Elkins Elroy rode his horse up a rutted dusty road the thirty miles from Pocatello to Lava Hot Springs. His sideburns were the shape of carpet cutter blades and his green eyes slightly bloodshot. He had just finished four years at Utah Agricultural College in Logan studying chemistry. He needed a long bath. He rode through town trying to remember what Logan had taught him. But as he thought he saw: sulphur used for rubber vulcanization and black gun powder – *that horse is bigger than Bessie but not near the trot* – rhombic melting point 112.8 – monoclinic 119 – boiling point 444.6 or 8 – *I'll slip in there for a beer and a pork sausage – damn there's women in this town* – Leibnitz really started it all with the ol'monads – *whoever thought of painting a hotel orange and green* – tubercle bacillus, rod-shaped, Mycobacterium tuberculosis – excuse me ma'am I'm sorry miss do they have pork sausage over there – *I'll be over at the spring if you have an inkling – she's shapely* – Pocatello ma'am miss but I like your town and that hawk circling the southerly pines.

He ate. It was seven by the time he dropped into the bubbling pool at the edge of town. He was alone and happy, eyes open, the world a shiny arch. He to walk through arch after arch, pool after pool, his world. He lay on his back, his head skyward. The steam around him met the darkening blue sky osmotically. Like under a microscope, the universe was flat, arched. Heaven just passed his nose. His legs lay suspended in the gurgle, the hairs conscious flagella. Sam felt his stomach, full of sausage and beer, weightless, floating to and fro in the bath.

For him everything fitted. For Sarah nothing did. She was viewing him from behind a branch of pine needles about twenty feet from the spring. She didn't know whether she should show herself, speak, whistle, or remain unknown. Sweet balls accumulated under her arms. She revised her hair. She wished she were one of the ants bumping heads on the trunk of the tree. She was twenty-six, the granddaughter of Mormon pioneers who'd been sent to settle Idaho, and in her virginity aching to unache.

When Apollo ascended from the waters Sarah rattled the pine needles. Sam pulled a towel around his waist and knew there was no wind that evening. He walked to Sarah and she followed him deeper into the woods. This was three months after Wilson in his inaugural had said: "This is not a day of triumph; it is a day of dedication. Here muster, not the forces of party, but the forces of humanity. Men's hearts wait upon us; men's lives hang in the balance; men's hopes call upon us to say what we will do … Who dares fail to try? God helping me, I will not fail…" Sam, coincidence or not, said, "It's a helluva nice evening, nice night to be out. And that bath gave me some special mustard I can feel simmering. I don't know 'bout you, but my heart's been dangling there in the middle of my chest and awaiting to burst. Man's gotta give sometime, don't he? Heaven help me… Let's sit down…" Water was dripping from the tips of his sideburns under his cheekbones. Night was enclosing.

Whether rape or not, it surely wasn't fun. Sarah clawed. She howled. She slugged. Then she gave a little. Then she clawed and howled. Then Sam got back what he had had before and a bit more. Sarah was like winter refusing the coming of spring. Blossoms appear then get smothered in a foot of snow. Then sun. Then snow. Spring did finally get through, tardily, messily. Too late for the waiting.

We all are conceived under some set of circumstances.

Ecce homo.

Ecce Martha.

*

Six people came to Martha's burial. She had made no plants or provisions for the occasion, so Elroy was left to do what he thought best. He decided on the midpoint between his and Bob Seaman's house. At five Saturday morning Wayne walked up the hill with a shovel and dug a hole the size of a garbage can. Elroy came up minutes later and said, "That should do it."

He set the time for 7am figuring the rest of the neighbours would be asleep or at least not past their coffee and San Francisco Chronicle. At ten to, just as the August sun threw a band of light across the dry eastern hills, Joan, Aaron, Rilda, and Helen Ruffenacht filed up to the hole. Grasshoppers bounced around their feet. Worms, some headed some beheaded, squirmed in the pile of fresh dirt next to the grave struggling to get back into darkness.

The six were silent, standing in a circle. Elroy sensed the cavity below was staring back up at them, an earth's eye getting a look at those who look. He looked up. He imagined the whole planet as a large eyeball gazing aimlessly at the moon, the stars, and the prism of space. Suddenly he said, "We forgot Martha."

They had. She was in a plastic container, like those used to transport cats on airplanes, in the closet in Elroy's bedroom. Martha had died in Switzerland. The authorities at the Embassy in Bern had wired Elroy whose name appeared on her passport as the individual to be notified in case of accident or death. With little time to think, Elroy wired back that Martha be cremated and the remains sent to Orinda. When the box arrived two weeks later Elroy took it into the bedroom, unwrapped and opened it. Fire had done to Martha what it would do to a bed or a table, though a few small chunks of bone were spared the reduction to ash. He ran his fingers through the cool grey rubble and thought lovingly of his sister. He was eight, she was twelve. They were still living in Pocatello. It was a winter day not long after Christmas. Elroy had received a new wooden sled. She was pulling him across fresh snow on an empty road. He turned and sat backwards on the sled and watched the tracks form in front of him as they went along. *"Faster! faster!"*he called and Martha ran. The naked elms lining the street were the silver castles of their kingdom. It began to snow and the traces of the sled were covered, leaving but two gentle threads pulling away in the distance.

Elroy closed up the box and put it under his sport coats in the closet.

Now he retrieved it and carried it back up the hill. Wayne helped him take off the lid. The circle enlarged slightly as Elroy lifted the container and poured his sister into the hole. A grey film hung in the air while the six inadvertently joined hands and bowed heads. Helen Ruffenacht said *bless you Martha,* then the group shuffled and walked down to the house. Wayne stayed behind to refill the grave. He remembered their black cat Willard and their dog Freddy were under there too, with the worms, not far from Martha.

*

Amber hadn't been there Saturday because she couldn't find a babysitter. She lived in Provo, a stone's throw from where her mother had been raised in Orem. Amber had spent two years at Brigham Young University majoring in men. A month into her third year she met Jerry who had just returned from Thailand where he'd laboured for two years trying to convert Buddhists to Mormonism. They were married over the Christmas break and now, five years later, had four children, a hamster, and a cornfield behind the house.

The Thursday after the Saturday, Amber sent this letter to her parents in California:

August 14, 1974

Dear Mom and Dad,

I'm sure sorry I couldn't be at Aunt Martha's funeral. Jerry had a closing and I just couldn't find a babysitter, but you know how much I loved Aunt Martha.

Thanks for remembering my birthday last week. It was kind of uneventful. I did go out to lunch with Ging and that was fun. We had Miles, but they were pretty good little boys, no running around with their cars or jumping under the booth and trying to eat the gum off the bottom the table, etc. Not yet anyway. Jerry had wall to wall apts, the whole day plus 2 or 3 that night, so we didn't get to do any celebrating, no cake, no opening presents, no happy birthday to you, etc. Actually we declared Saturday my "pretend birthday" as the kids called it, and I made myself a cake, and then we opened presents that the kids got me and that Jerry got me and it was fun. Ging did bring me a piece of delicious carrot cake with a candle in it that she had made. On the night of my birthday I felt like I needed to do some kind of celebrating so I took Richelle to the Varsity Theater to see a movie that the BYU operator said was a kind of romance mystery. Turns out it was the stupidest movie about Chinatown and a truck driver that I've ever seen with lots of gang war and fighting among different Chinese gangs, etc. Richelle promptly spilled her popcorn, which I tried to pick up off the floor, and in a half hour we left. That was fine with her as she didn't get it anyway.

I had kind of a wild day on Monday. I took the Falcon in to get snow tires put on it. Not that there's any snow, but we figured since the regular tires were pretty worn, we'd put on the snow tires to use them up a little instead of using up the regular tires. So I sit there 15 minutes wrestling with Bradley. I can't even read a magazine, as he attacks everything and wrinkles it up and shoves it in his mouth. As I'm sitting there I watch a man get in his car to drive away that they've just finished working on and as he drives less than a block, his tire falls off and the car tips onto the axle? Great work at this place, right? He was pretty disgusted. I mentioned this to Clixie and she said the exact thing happened to her husband at the same place. Don't trust them with your tires. Anyway, after sitting there for 15 minutes the guy comes and tells me that he can't put on the snow tires as they're legally bald and it's against the law (Good thing Jerry's got all his hair – Yuk! yuk!). Kind of made me feel like a parolee or something. So that was a wasted trip. When I got home, Jerry runs off to an apt, and then shortly thereafter, Frank, Nina's husband, shows up for his apt with Jerry so he's sitting in the living room and then a guy comes over to sign a lease on the building, so both he and Frank are here in my living room and then the phone keeps ringing, and Bradley wakes up and then Andy and his friends come racing through the living room with guns and karate chops, etc. Kind of wild, but luckily it all calmed down after a while. Why does everything always happen at once? Then Tom called, but I was glad to talk to him since I'd just signed a lease and he was thrilled and overjoyed, so that was fun.

I went to lunch with Clixie on Wednesday to a Japanese restaurant that she loves but I kind of didn't like all the slimy stuff and the bean curd, etc. in my dish of whatever it was. We had a fun time though, again, I brought Bradley and had Andy play at a friend's and Richelle was in preschool. As soon as we finished lunch we went across a street to Wool-worth's 10 cent sale and I got some party favors etc. They had panties on sale so I got some for the girls, and a pair of 2 dollar slippers for Andy that he was absolutely thrilled with. Course that very night the seam in the front came out, so I sewed it and they're perfectly fine now. When I got home Kathi arrived and we talked for a while and then went to Sees Candy, but got waylaided at a new custard store and she bought me a big malt that was wonderful and we skipped Sees Candy.

Last Thursday two birds slammed into my picture window while I was on the phone to Gail and one died. It was quite dramatic, and I explained it all to the kids who saw him lying there. Then Jerry buried him the next day.

Friday I went up to Salt Lake to an eye doctor apt. They have a place up there, Gail went to it, that's kind of like a compact warehouse place. I ordered two pairs and got the eye exam all for 39.95. Can't beat that as I pay 65 just for one pair of contacts here with no eye exam. Only problem was it took two hours and I had the three youngest kids! Horrors. They made me move 5 different times to 5 different rooms so it was a major move each time, loading and unloading, blankets, diaper bags, toys, purses, etc. I was so happy to finally get out of there.

Mom, I was reading your life story this past week and found it really interesting that all the traits you mentioned we had as babies are still with us today. It was incredible. Also when I finished Grandma Hatch's life story I turned out the light (Jerry was already in bed) and laid in bed and sobbed. Jerry couldn't understand what was wrong. I explained to him that I just felt like I really missed Grandma and I remembered how hard it had been for her at the end, and that poem you put in just tore my heart out. You surely did an excellent job on all those histories. The wall papering experience sounded hideous!

Tonight in Family Hour since I have my darling FH chart, Tara's assignment was to give the lesson, so she and Jerry chose baptism, got out my file with stories on baptism and proceeded to read a story on the flip chart and then asked the kids questions. Well, Andy and Richelle's attention span is never very good when they hear someone reading along very fast in kind of a monotone, so that didn't go over real big as it is. Then when she asked them questions like, "Who did Joseph Smith see when he prayed in the grove?" Andy said, "the President of the United States." Then every question Tara asked Richelle about baptism, her answer was "the United States!" I almost died with laughter.

Hope everything went fine at the funeral.

Well, time to flip out the light. Love Amber.

Elroy sipped a beer between his daughter's paragraphs. Between words, inside Joe Garagiola's rendition of Saturday morning baseball, he silently thanked Amber, Adolph Coors, and Mr. Garagiola for sealing Martha safely inside the hill behind his house. He went outside and trimmed the rhododendrons, swept the back patio, and burned the trash in the incinerator. When he was sure the fire wasn't going anywhere he walked up to Bob Seaman's house and dove clothed past the 8' mark into his friend's backyard pool.

Elroy was an inventor. He started his career while in the FBI. He used to watch the janitor sweep out the office in Baltimore. The janitor, a raw Polish immigrant with conic ears named Georges Wyspianski, would sweep all the papers, dust, paperclips and candy wrappers into a large pile in the centre of the office. He did this with a large push broom. Then he would fetch an old metal dustpan and a small hand broom, get down on his knees and pick up the mess, putting it little by little into a big cardboard box which he would carry to the garbage bin. Elroy observed the man dutifully duplicate the process every night.

Elroy liked Wyspianski and often invited him across the street for a beer if they finished at the same time. They communicated with winks, smiles, frowns, and a few syllabicated repetitive sounds. Their shared understanding was proportional to their intake of beer. Elroy wanted to do more for his friend than just buy him drink. One evening, with a hive of bottles on the red and white checked tablecloth in front of them, Elroy hit on his first creation. He slapped the janitor on the back and raised his glass. "Georgie," he declared, "sweeping will never be the same."

Wyspianski started guzzling down beer not knowing exactly why.

Elroy's revelation was a long flat strip of plastic. It would have a groove and could be attached to any big cardboard box. It would be called "The Big Edge" or "The Jumbo Dustpan" and would eliminate the need to exchange the large push broom for the small hand model. The same broom could be used to push the swept pile into a box thanks to the plastic edge. By the time Elroy got the first 10,000 off the assembly line he was long out of the FBI, but he sent five to Wyspianski with his fondest greetings and memories.

The timing of the invention was perfect as the post-war era put thousands of families in suburban homes, millions of children on patios and driveways, and even more shrubs along sidewalks leading to front doors, all resulting in piles to be conquered with Elroy's edge. Elroy put an ad in *Parade Magazine* and within two weeks *THE BIG EDGE* swept the nation. Success was most pronounced in the Midwest, Utah, Oregon, California and certain parts of the Northeast. Only New York was slow to bite. Elroy made two hundred and forty thousand dollars before people finally got tired of large boxes with lime green edges cluttering their garages and sheds, and the small metal dustpan was once again the American preference. The money took the Elroys to California and nestled them into a four-bedroom home on Lombardy Lane.

Whereas his first invention resulted from his warm heart, Elroy's second was a response to a cold back. He had just played the third round of a mixed-doubles tennis tournament at the Orinda Club. He came home and filled the bathtub with hot water. It was 1956. The twins were seven and were in their room next to the bathroom singing, *Whistle while you work, Stevenson's a jerk, Eisenhower has more power, and he does more work.* Elroy dropped his tennis shorts and slipped into the water. His legs sunk into warmth, but his back hit the cold exposed upper part of the tub. The shot of chill along his spine far outweighed the initial pleasant sensation of warmth. *This needn't be*, Elroy thought. Before he had soaped his washcloth the *CHILL-Y-OUT TUB* was alive and growing to the left of the sagital groove in Elroy's skull.

The tubs came in cream, lavender, aqua blue, and pink. A thin coil inside the porcelain was activated when the water was turned on and heated the tub wall opposite the spout to eighty-seven degrees within two minutes. The first actual domestic installation was in the Elroy house five years later, a few days after the outbreak of the Bay of Pigs crisis. They sold well in suburban California, oddly where the weather was warmest. Elroy understood this to mean that southern residents of the state abhorred cold in every form except that which went in the mouth.

CHILL-Y-OUT wasn't the financial success that *THE BIG EDGE* had been, but it kept Elroy on the tennis courts and golf courses and the family fed until Martha strolled onto the plane that would take her to Zurich.

*

In the salmon Cadillac, Elroy drove Martha from Concord to the San Francisco airport. Her suitcase sat next to the spare tyre in the trunk. Oddly it didn't bulge, containing only a pair of polyester pyjamas, a frayed grey suit, a beige cotton blouse, eight pairs of opaque nylon stockings, an apricot mohair cardigan with a hole in the right sleeve, six pairs of heavy cotton underpants, a skirt with printed palm trees, blue fluff slippers, a maroon shawl, a grey plastic raincoat, the Duchess of Chartres, a pair of thick brown shoes, six packs of juju drops, and a pair of wool socks with a hundred dollar bill in each toe. In the car she wore her paisley dress with newly sewn pockets on the inside packed with twenties, fifties, and hundreds. The ones, fives, and tens were in her brassiere and shoes. Her handbag contained her passport, Kleenex, a pack of jujus, and a chain of keys to places past.

The Cadillac purred between green April hills then plunged into the Caldecott Tunnel. They crossed the Bay Bridge and skirted the heart of San Francisco.

"We're going to miss you," Elroy said.

"Not a soul in those skyscrapers knows I breathe."

"Joan and I and the kids."

"Good," she said. "I don't know what I'll miss, but who knows, Elroy, it might be you. Maybe the plane won't get off the ground. If there's one thing I've learned it's don't fry your brains thinking about what's going to be. I laid out a whole life with a guy named Ray Hiller, married him, kissed him under a green hat, then never saw his ass again."

"Where do you land?"

"Zurich, somewhere in Sweden."

"I think that's Switzerland, Martha."

"What's the difference? Zurich is Zurich. I just told the guy to get me a ticket to Europe. The ticket doesn't say anything about Sweland or Swissland. It says Zurich. You got a map, look at it. I don't." They drove by Candlestick Park, a big empty bowl, no cherries, no packers.

"Write us and tell us where you are."

"Sure Elroy. Listen I just want to tell you that *that* Thanksgiving I was doing what I had to do and so were you so one plus one is one. My fingers don't quite bend right, but other than that no skin off anybody's toes, right?"

Elroy turned off the freeway and followed the departure signs. Martha was on a non-stop Balair charter flight. They stopped at the curb in front of international departures and Elroy unloaded the suitcase.

"I'll park and be right back to see you off," the brother said.

"Thanks, Elroy, but I'm already gone so there's really no need."

They hugged profoundly. Elroy closed his eyes and envisioned his sister – arms flapping and paisley flowers rippling – winging her way past San Mateo, out over the Pacific, then curving back above the Golden Gate before finally disappearing, feet last, into a billow of cement clouds. They unclenched. Brother wept. No porters. Martha lugged her suitcase into the terminal.

H3 was an aisle seat, Martha's. H2 was occupied by a girl in her early twenties with small wire rim glasses, a part down the middle of her head, and a t-shirt announcing "The Grateful Dead" covering her loose chest. The girl smelled of incense. Martha asked her if it was her first time in an airplane.

"Well not really," the girl said, "like the ol'man's got a small job that we used to scoot to Palm Springs in, ya know like when it was raining and shit, but if you mean like a big jobber, yeah, I guess you could say I'll be flyin' high primo, if you dig?"

When they got up in the air the girl took a small wad of tinfoil out of her jeans pocket. She pried it open and flipped into her mouth what looked to Martha to be a pellet of rabbit dung.

"If you don't mind me asking, what was that?" Martha inquired.

"Sorry baby, like I'd slip you some but my boyfriend only had one number. That's what he said anyway." The girl must have identified with Martha's unkempt hair. "No pigs up here. Like if you think about it, since there's no pigs and narcs in moonland like we could bring out the pipe and toke all the way to Tokyo."

"You mean we stop in Tokyo first?"

"No baby, like I was just letting the words do their thing."

"But what were you eating?"

"That was just a chunk of hash cause Jocko, you know, Jocko he's my man, said like I should take off before the plane does to make the trip fly – you know like trip through the trip – but I figured I'd better not toke in the airport so I ate it here. Listen, I'm Mandy," the girl offered, putting forth a hand littered with lead-looking rings.

"I'm Martha."

"Right on, Martha…Like I had an aunt named Martha but I ain't seen 'er since Joan of Arc invaded Poland. I'm from Berkeley, I mean I had a pad in the Haight but it got too heavy so I slipped across the bay one night when my boyfriend was like really stoned and I met Jocko like on the first night when I was looking for a place to crash."

Martha had trouble understanding the girl but explained she had lived in Concord and now intended to live somewhere else but she didn't know where.

"You mean like you just said up yours to Trickie Dickie and split. Well that's some heavy shit. Me, I'm meetin' a couple of friends in Amsterdam then like we're gunna hitchhike around, ya know, blow in the wind a while and check out the Europe scene for like a month then head back to the pad."

The flight attendant came by with drinks. Martha asked for tomato juice and fished a dollar out her bra.

"There's no charge ma'am," the flight attendant said lowering peanuts and a gin and tonic to the hippie's fold-out tray. Hippie: circa 1965; species unbathed, uncut, unsnapped, unduly, unemployed, ununderweared underneath, untied, underfed, unbidden, unlicensed, uncrowned, unzipped.

"Could you slip me a couple more packs of them peanuts?" Mandy asked. When the attendant mechanically obliged, Martha raised a finger and was rewarded with a second tomato juice. Martha said thank you and the cart was pushed to the next row of passengers.

Mandy threw handful after handful of peanuts into her mouth. "Doesn't Jocko feed you?" Martha asked.

"Just got the munchies, honey."

After the meal Martha slept soundly through the shortened night. When she woke the seatbelt sign was on and the plane, now under a thick mat of clouds that had glided down from the Arctic, was descending on Zurich.

The hippie had made Martha feel good, that she belonged, that she was going where she ought to be going. After clearing passport control she found a restroom to relieve her bladder. She locked herself behind a grey door that extended from ceiling to floor. She hung her purse on the hook on the backside of the door. The black seat glinted, the bowl was clean. As Martha lifted her dress and squirmed to lower her underclothes, a shower of bills – 20s, 50s and 100s – released and floated randomly to the floor. She squatted onto the bowl and winked affectionately at Grant, Jackson, and Franklin. Each in his turn winked back.

"I like your shoes," Grant said.

"Do you?" Martha said shyly. "I got them at Sears at the January Clearance Sale. Actually Mr. Grant…"

"Please, call me Ulysses."

"Yes. Actually Ulysses, I hesitated between these and a blue pair with bows, but for the trip I thought these would be nicer."

"What strikes me is the way your feet appear so at rest, no wrinkles of skin nor unseemly fatty bulges near the toes and ankles."

"You noticed, Mr. President?"

"Ulysses."

"Ulysses."

"And though your stockings permit me not a look at your calves, I would guess, judging from their shape, that they are firm and show few unsightly veins considering you age."

"You flatter me," Martha said with eyelids dancing.

"Had I known we were to meet I would have dressed differently or at least worn my spectacles."

"Who needs spectacles when lavender radiates from milady as from spring's first flower?" It was Franklin interrupting from where he had come to rest under the toilet paper. Martha wiggled her thighs and brushed back her hair exposing the left half of her neck.

"Ah! But then sight and scent together yield even greater dividends."

A small fly pounced on Franklin's nose then took aim on a cornered cigarette butt where it made a safe landing.

"Keep your nose out of this, or I'll call in the cavalry." Grant interjected.

"*Cher collègue*," Franklin said calmly, "if there is nothing else *au fond de notre société*, there is at least the endowed freedom for a woman to catch the man of her choosing, for her choosing, and by her choosing. And if milady's intelligence is in any way commensurate to her beauty, her choice will hardly be more difficult than peeling a tomato."

"Cut the shit, Ben," Jackson chided from his side of the floor. "I've had my eye on this woman for longer than it takes a bullfrog to rip a fart and I'm not about to lose her to your sophomoric rhetoric."

"Mr. Jackson, I had no idea…" Martha mumbled softly. She batted at the toilet paper to lower a few sheets and in so doing blew Franklin toward the wall.

"*Mon Dieu! Il y a des currents d'air!*"

"Listen Ben, that French stuff might work back east, but Martha here is from Pocatello where men talk like men and not like peacocks with plugged nostrils." Jackson eyed Martha's lips, creased high to low but succulent like finally sliced tomatoes. "Miss Martha, when a mouth beckons I reckon that a union must and shall be created."

"If I can slip in a word between these two pockets of hot air," Grant huffed, "it was I who first engaged Martha's tongue on the subject of her shoes tastefully selected at the January Clearance and it is I who will escort her from her throne when her stately business reaches its end."

"*Tu parles*," Franklin said.

"Horseshit," Jackson said.

Martha lifted the front of her dress and tenderly wiped herself one time. She leaned forward and with delicate fingers gathered her money. She folded the wad, slid it past her cleavage and burrowed it under her smiling bosom. She rose, flushed, retrieved her handbag, pulled the grey door, and wandered – as only she could wander – to the baggage claim area.

When she got there a number of minutes later, a man in an airport uniform was taking the lone remaining suitcase from the revolving black belt. It was Martha's. She ran toward him twirling her arms.

"Drop it, señor!" she shouted, whacking the man's wrist with her purse. He jumped back in surprise.

"*Bitte, Fräulein, bitte, beruhigen Sie sich.*"

"Yeah, bit a', bit a', you almost lost a bit a your filthy paw. Now gimme my suitcase!" Martha examined the man and realized he was an employee and not a thief. She softened, "Actually I wouldn't mind a bit of breakfast. Know any Sambo's or anything around here?"

"*Verzeihen Sie, ich spreche nicht English.*" The man excused himself with a slight bow. Martha walked toward a green door marked NICHTS ZU VERZOLLEN but was accosted by another gentleman in a pale uniform.

"And what do *you* want?" Martha piped. "Listen, three presidents and José over there and I'm not even out of the airport."

"I will to ask you if you have somsing to declare," he said politely.

"Yeah, I declare I'd like somesing to eat. You guys are all real nice an all but dinner was about two days ago and I musta slept through breakfast. In fact join me if you want, but point me toward somebody's kitchen." The customs officer smiled. He had a dark brown moustache trimmed at the lip and eyebrows that met above his nose. His teeth were stained but otherwise he looked healthy.

"Sis must be your first holiday in Europe," he said.

"Is that where I am? Listen, it's been a pleasure and all but I think I'll be on my way." Martha trudged through the green electric door. The officer said *d'amis* and did nothing to stop her.

She left the terminal building. It was snowing lightly. The air smelled perfumed like cut grass. Martha set her suitcase on a bench and took out her apricot sweater and plastic raincoat. She fought the cold with what she had, but she felt sticky, her scalp itched, and her insides growled.

She had not seen snow since 1959 when one February morning two inches fell on Concord. She left the *I Love Lucy Show* and stood outside her backdoor to watch pyracantha, junipers, gravel, and stubby straw fields turn white. She heard Lucy and Desi shout at each other and they were white too. She stared in and stared out and saw Elroy, just after his eighth birthday, in white being dunked into a white baptismal basin while the Father, Son, and Holy Ghost nodded approval at the mention of their names in their white robes with their white beards brushing their chests.

It was Easter Sunday and she in white new dress with an embroidered rose on the collar sat next to her mother who was not white like she was when she lay like a bleached wax fruit in her coffin, but was proud and pink. And Elroy rose from the water with the whitest soul but now white was free to choose dirt or snow and dirt was hell and snow was heaven.

Then they came home from church and Martha in her dress on the toilet doing a difficult number two and Elroy rushing in saying he had to do number one and couldn't wait and if she didn't get off he'd pee on her which he did yellowing her dress.

She was dirty, but was he? He was dry and white and she was wet and dirty so she asked her Father-in-Heaven why only she was dirty. She didn't get an answer. The pyracantha, junipers, gravel, and straw fields were white until three-thirty when *Queen For A Day* came on and the snow became water and seeped into the earth.

The snow clung to the taxis lined up outside the Kloten Airport. It fell in big wet chips that dropped like diving birds. Martha looked up and tried to follow the flight of single flakes. Did the snow fall faster in solitary than collectively? When she was able to keep her eye on one flake the sidewalk jumped to catch it.

She shivered in her raincoat and California shoes. The blue ones with the white bows would have been no better suited for the weather that now absorbed her. She pulled her suitcase to the curb and climbed into a taxi. It was a Mercedes with a back seat big enough for a family. The driver, a stooped old man in a down coat, spoke no English. Martha explained she itched and wanted, more than food, a hot bath. She repeated the words "hot bath" and "bath hot" a half dozen times. The only sound that lodged in the driver's ear was a variant of "bath hot", for him "Bahnhof", so he took her to the train station. The meter said 14.80 and Martha, in no mood for an argument, gave the man 15 dollars. He unloaded the suitcase and bowed reverentially dipping his head and catching snowflakes on the back of his neck.

The air was cooling, the snow changed. It was whiter and thicker. The sky had disappeared. Martha was standing in front of the entrance to the station opposite the Bahnhofstrasse, but she didn't know it. She had eloped with Cadillac, plane, and taxi, to a sidewalk under a blizzard. Momentarily her brain froze. No thought of her need for: the new footwear, coat, language, food, friend, or bath; no thought of her need for the past: Elroys, Concord, Hiller, Ruffenacht, Navarro, Pocatello, Lucy, years counted by ones. She stared down Bahnhofstrasse like down a steel tube. She wasn't cold. She didn't itch. *Redemptio. Redemptus. Redimere.* Snow crawled up her ankles. She was nowhere and didn't know where nowhere was. Globs of ice crystals settled in her hair. Her eyelashes were frosted, congealed like her brain. Snow piled on her suitcase.

A person doesn't freeze to death in front of a train station of a large city at eleven o'clock in the morning. Before the statue cracks somebody will intervene.

"Lady, like I don't like to stick my nose in other people's shit, but if you don't get your ass in gear you're gonna be fuckin Frosty-the-Snowman's wife. I'm all for transmed and shit, but the gurus I know never recommended sitting in a freezer…I mean what the fuck, lady, are you alright?"

It was Mandy hunched under backpack in a pink parka and a Peruvian bonnet. She didn't recognise Martha but she was the only person on the continent Martha would have recognised.

"Mandy." Martha moved.

"Huh – well I'll be a horse's butthole! It's you again! Where the hell you goin'? I mean whataya doin' standin' here like an Eskeemo? You best git your hide inside before your boobies fall off."

"Where am I?" Martha asked, lips corrugated.

"Where are ya! Like if I'd known this shit I'd a never let you off the plane alone. Come on sweetheart, Mandy's gonna git Martha set up."

Mandy grabbed the suitcase and Martha's icy hand. As they limped toward the restaurant inside the lugubrious station, Martha said, "I'm happy."

*

Elroy took the back way home from the airport. He drove south on 101 and crossed the San Mateo Bridge. He looped through Fremont, Sunol, Pleasanton, and Danville on 680. Traffic was sparse. He had a slight erection, as if his body were telling him tears can pass through a third duct or that blood detoured from the brain can carry sorrow with it. He hadn't tried nor wanted to dissuade Martha from her trip, but the truth was she didn't know where she was going. Whose tears were shed for Columbus?

His erection drooped like an unwatered rose where 680 met 34. Instead of turning for Orinda, he stayed on 680 for Concord.

Brother turned off on Willow Pass Road and drove to sister's home. That morning was long before. Martha had waited at the street corner for Elroy's car. When it came she waved to Elroy then turned and waved to her house of thirty years. When they drove off she turned and waved again.

On the doorstep Elroy squib-kicked an issue of the *Contra Costa Times*. The front entrance was locked. He leapfrogged sister's patch of petunias and petticoat narcissi and took the path to the back. The door was ajar. Martha didn't have a bedroom, sitting-room, and kitchen – she had a room with a bed, another with a sofa and one with the Westinghouse refrigerator. Otherwise everything overlapped: near the bed a big orange armchair and a cupboard filled with dry beans, canned cherries, tomato juice, and magazines; contiguous to the sofa was a table with stacks of plates, a five-gallon tin of wheat, a pair of gardening gloves, a trowel, and a Japanese bathrobe; the refrigerator was surrounded by a small armchair, reading lamp, cupboard with shoes below and foodstuffs and cleaning materials above, a two-burner hotplate, and a wicker rake. The television was on a rolling cart to move it from room to room. Were Martha home this day she should have watched *The Price Is Right, Concentration, As The World Turns, I Love Lucy, Let's Make A Deal,* and *Queen For A Day.* After the sun went down she rarely had the set on. Something about the lighted machine in a dark world made her afraid, or lonely, or both.

Elroy had spent little time in her home. Thanksgivings, birthdays, and Christmas he would pick her up in the Cadillac. Other than Mrs. Ruffenacht's, the fingerprints in the room were entirely Martha's.

Brother inhaled sister.

The postcards on the refrigerator door were from no one. He pulled the handle. There was a six-pack of beer with a note attached.

Dear Elroy,

You'll find this before you find me. I love you.

Martha.

Brother wept, wilted.

Sister chewed croissants with Mandy.

*

In early afternoon the snow stopped. The clouds broke into chunks and the sun intermittently glazed the city. They changed money, then put backpack and suitcase in a station locker. Mandy led Martha across the street to buy a coat and boots. The snow was six inches deep on Bahnhofstrasse. The shop windows were full of silver, copper, and vanilla mannequins outfitted for spring. Blue and yellow were in this season. Slender bodies wore aquamarine dresses with bright canary flowers, sapphire suits above lemon high heels, indigo skirts and blouses printed with tiger swallowtails and honeysuckle. Umbrellas were yellow as were children's galoshes and tablecloths. Men's wear tended toward blue with amethystine traces in sweaters and ties. An early April snowfall was not abnormal – winters seemed to be arriving later – yet the store owners rubbed spring in their customers' faces.

They entered a cheap-looking department store named ABM where Martha found an army-green parka (green had been the designer's choice for winter) on sale for fifty-nine francs. She paid the cashier, inspecting her change as an animal lover examining a sparrow that had died in the hand. In the shoe department she got a pair of olive fur-lined boots that zipped up the side.

"Grab a gun and you're Captain Martha!" Mandy said outside.

"Do you like my coat?"

"Hey, you look like a Siberian princess."

"You said 'Captain'…"

"Captain! Princess! Shitless! What the hell's the difference? Like what it is is that Martha here looks like the doc just flushed out the ol' blood and pumped in some king's juice. Ya warm?"

"I feel fine. Thanks. You know I haven't seen snow in ten years." Miniature clouds surrounded their heads as they talked.

"Dig."

"Dig."

"Hi digger."

At the end of Bahnhofstrasse in a small park they made a snowman. Wind blew sheets of glitter from the trees. Children threw snowballs at them. Captain Martha attacked back.

From Bürkliplatz they crossed a bridge at the join where lake meets river. Cakes of snow muffled the tyres of passing cars. Martha observed the lake thinking it must be that other ocean. Walkers in conversation passed talking in hoarse cackling sounds – she imagined their ancestors hunched over fires in dark caves blowing ferociously at dying cinders. Was it a language born of a struggle to keep warm? Had her fellow pedestrians fled dead fires? Was the Duchess of Chartres painted with frosted fingers? She remembered the postcards on her refrigerator – blue sky, majestic castles, tuliped gardens. Had she got off the plane too soon?

They walked along Limmat-Quai next to the river and crossed Rathaus Bridge. Martha's boots lifted the loose snow; her feet were warm, thighs rubbing under her paisley dress chilled like metal slabs. They wandered through narrow streets that didn't have horse-drawn sleighs, but might have, pulling couples in mink garments – man moustached, woman pink-cheeked – toward a radiant drawing room filled with cavaliers, swelled gowns, and distant violins. Martha in sequined satin with bosoms high, lifting her hand, thumb curled under, accepting Navarro's kiss and spinning *one-two-three* neath chandelier shimmer. *Fair Lord consume me. All Concord prays it. One-two-three. I count infinity's stars.*

Mandy took Martha's arm on the downgrades.

"When are you meeting your friends?"

"When we've both had a bath or it snows black, whichever comes first."

"Are they expecting you?"

"Yeah, like my parents were expecting me."

"Your parents?"

"Like my mother didn't expect me til she saw her gizzard balloon, then she expected me only cause like she had to expect me. And the ol'man never expected anything cause the ol'man pulled a hit and run. Then when I was ten he came back to pick up the pieces. Me and Mama were livin' Vegas – it wasn't bad, we had this house out by the golf course and Mama used to say if you can't get a job in Vegas you can't get a job. She had this French boyfriend Jacques who I thought was my father until the real one showed up. Mama never really said yes or no about Jacques – I guess she figured I was too little either way – so when the ol'man drives up one day in a Ferrari or sumpin' and hugs me up callin' me angel pie all hell breaks loose. Mama took me into the garage and turned the car radio on real loud that was playin' *Ain't Nuin But A Hound Dog*. Finally the ol'man comes in with a rose tucked behind his ear and declares the creation of a human family. My guess is that no other bitch gave him a kid so there I am – the one and only – screwin's ugly duck – flyin' between Mars and Venus. So we all up and move to Yuba City where Daddy's got these apple orchards..."

"What did Jacques do?"

"He carved up the meat at the buffet at the Tropicana."

"I mean what happened to him?"

"I think he's still at the Tropicana. Anyway, Yuba City was cool except when the river used to flood and shit. Once I saw our pad on the 6 o'clock news with this car floating by. But I kinda flipped out in high school – like when I was a freshman I wouldn't take showers at gym cause my boobies were plums and some of these chicks were sportin' watermelons and the teacher – Miss Tye – used give me demerits like shit cause showers were a school rule. Then when I was a junior my locker was next to this hole named Juliette Olmstead who campaigned for pom-pom girl between her legs and so the day of the selection I came to school with ten Trojans blown up with helium by a guy at the carnival and wrote *Bedstead For Omstead* and *Up Trojans* on 'em. I walked across the quad givin' out the balloons and singin' *One little, two little, three little Trojans. Four little, five little, six little Trojans…*I thought it was pretty damn funny, but I got suspended for a week. The dean told me it was people like me that made America dirty. Actually after it all blew over Juliette and I got to be good friends – in fact she's one of the girls in Amsterdam…"

"When are you going?"

"Loosen the noose, honey…What happened was like we met at the lockers one day and she starts yellin' and callin' me a slimy salamander so I pulled the shit out of her hair and she said 'uncle' and started cryin' and said she only did it because she thought she was ugly – and I mean the chick was nice – cause her old man kept sayin' that since as long as she could remember. Like then I knew she was for real and not a slut so we ended up real tight. I used to watch her pom-pom at basketball games and think here's this beautiful girl some people think is a whore and others take for the Virgin Mary and she's out there shakin' the shit out of her buns cause her ol'man's a dick."

At six-thirty they were back at Bürkliplatz. The snow was chopped and crusted. Pink stripes disappeared in the blackening sky. The lake hissed and held the cold. They went across the bridge to Bellevueplatz and got a room at the Hotel Otter. By nine they were both bathed and asleep, Martha in her Penney's polyester pyjamas curled on a small wooden bed, Mandy mouth opened in a muted snore in her High Sierra sleeping bag, naked under the window, face warmed by a yellow moon.

*

Moe is the new music teacher at an elite girl's school where all the flowers wear round-neck cashmere sweaters, plaid skirts, and patent leather shoes. The headmistress – spectacled, hair in bun, large behind and chest – greets him with much ado. He bows, smiles, disguising chaos that simmers in the wing. Girls snicker at the sight of a man. Larry and Curly appear. Heads bopped, noses torn, fingers snap and flap. Lesson begins: Moe's Symphony.

B – O – Bo, B – I – Bi, B – I – Bickeby, B – O – Bo, Bicky – Bi Bo Bi Bo Bu Bicky Bi Bo Bu, L – I – Li, L – O – Lo, L – I – Licky Li – L – O – Lo, Licky – Li – Lo – Le – Lo – Lu – Licky – Li – Lo – Lu, M – I – Mi – M – O – Mo, M – I – Mickymi – M – O – Mo, Micky – mi – Mo – me – Mo – Mu – Micky – Mi – Mo – Me.

Girls fidget with delight, delicate petals. Curly and Larry, puppies in heat, dig the dirt while Moe waves the wand. Headmistress, feigning castration, struts and flails. Purity in danger.

Elroy is on his third beer. He has moved the TV into Martha's kitchen. Twilight dims the house.

The symphony gets through letters J and K before opposing forces finally collide. The girls jostle. The headmistress stomps shaking mountainous butt. The stooges flee, dropping the pollen count to zero.

Elroy drives home grinning.

Joan has made a pot roast with onions, carrots, and potatoes. She smells beer, husband's perfume. Husband smells pot roast, his favourite meal.

Wife ignores perfume of beer because her husband is a good man and doesn't drive drunk.

God ignores Elroy because tickets to good seats in Celestial Kingdome don't go to beer fans, they say.

Elroy doesn't ignore God because he is sitting in the chapel, Orinda Ward, Walnut Creek Stake, under Salt Lake's halo. Joan sits to his right, her hand affectionately nestled on his tweed jacket between his bicep and his ribs. The meeting opens with Brother Farnsworth's prayer. He expresses thanks for a few things – the nice day, the Sabbath that brings us together, the leaders of the congregation and those in Salt Lake, the opportunity to worship, the free land that we live in; he asks God to bless things – those who are sick or afflicted and could not be here this day, the missionaries in the field, the leaders of the Church, and us that we might get closer to Him; he says amen in Jesus Christ's name. Elroy enjoys the prayer – he likes Brother Farnsworth – but he thinks of what has been omitted. If we are talking to God should we just talk about what's on our block? What about Wyspianski? Martha's petunias? Singapore? Jupiter? Needn't we remember that the universe is big? Elroy wants to give the prayer one day and say thank You for all that is, bless all that is, and amen in the name of all that is, but beer keeps him from pulpit. This doesn't bother him because he thinks it wouldn't matter.

Brother Farnsworth leaves the pulpit to sit with his family. He is replaced by Bishop Farnell. He welcomes the congregation and announces the programme, and reminds the brothers and sisters that the Ward Bazaar is Friday night, that the Ward Basketball Team finished second, and that Sister Sprewer's Funeral will be held here in the chapel Wednesday at 2 p.m.

The opening song is *We Thank Thee O God for a Prophet*. Joan squeezes Elroy's bicep. Her spine tingles. The song says, "We thank Thee O God for a Prophet to guide us in these latter days". Latter days? Elroy hopes the days are not lattering. He rethinks his prayer to include all that has been and will be; every speck of the universe should be blessed. Voices resound joyfully; where is the joy in the final destruction? But, Elroy thinks, nary a singer's mind is on Armageddon. Music more important than words. Sound tingles more spines than ink.

Bishop Farnell announces Brother Fairchild.

"My Brothers and Sisters, it's a pleasure to be here with you today and to share the warmth and spirit of this congregation. I want to thank Bishop Farnell for giving me this opportunity to address you. I want to address the subject of faith, because faith in these latter days is the key to our eternal and lasting salvation… Just yesterday I was having my car washed at a fundraiser for the Little League team over at the Shell station. Now there were four little leaguers working on my car and each one was devoted to his work and my car in a different way. One boy left grease on the hubcaps. Another forgot a square fourth of the roof. The third boy was rubbing the hood at a snail's pace. Then there was the fourth boy – he worked like a pioneer. His windows were spotless, and he did the chrome too and it shone like… like… like a crystal ball. His work was a function of the faith he had in his parents, his church, and his Saviour. And that fourth boy was little Johnny Larsen sitting right here with his family on the fifth row (Johnny blushes, parents beam). When I saw what faith can do for a twelve-year-old, then I knew what the prophets said when they said faith can move mountains… Faith in your shammy is the key to a clean car. Faith in your mind is the key to a clean body. Faith in your wife is the key to a happy marriage. Faith in the Lord Jesus Christ is the key to everlasting eternal salvation. May we all be inspired by little Johnny Larsen and build bridges of faith across which we can drive clean cars into the Kingdom of God…

"I say these things humbly in the name of Jesus Christ, Amen."

Elroy says amen. Fairchild's warmth is more important than his words. Fairchild drives an old Rambler and his wife died eight years ago.

Elroy is more important than the beer he drinks.

He goes to heaven.

He loves.

*

She dreams.

Martha.

The moon has moved and the earth has moved. The moon now glows in somebody else's window.

She boards a waiting bus in Oakland at the station on Telegraph Avenue. The bus is an enlarged black-green slug.

The bus pulls out of the station slug-like; it actually pulls itself. Martha is going to visit Hiller, Raymond, private in the U.S. Army, Camp Pendleton. He has a weekend leave and has booked a room in a motel on the beach in Del Mar.

In the slug it takes nine hundred days to get from Oakland to Del Mar: ten months to Fresno, another ten from Fresno to Bakersfield, four months to climb over the mountains from Bakersfield to Los Angeles, and a final hundred fifty days to eke down the coast.

Martha enjoys the ride; she sees a California never seen, inch by inch. Any impatience to see her husband and lover is kept in check until the slug slug-pulls into Newport Beach. Newport is not yet swank; Martha sees two normal untanned people holding hands on the boardwalk. Her heart inflates painfully. As the couple kisses in front of a huge crackling white wave, her heart breaks through her ribs and floats into the blue sky. It is on a string that Martha holds in her hand as she sits in the slug. The slug window is down. She ties the string to her ring finger between the phalange and her wedding band. For a sleepless month she watches her heart dance and jerk like a kite a half a mile above the Pacific.

The bus slug-pulls into Del Mar. Ray is waiting at the station wearing only swim fins. He flip-flaps to her, embraces her and whispers, "I love you for being you."

It rains blood.

Martha thinks she has screamed but she hasn't. She turns on the lamp above her bed and fumbles for her watch. It says four. She thinks it is afternoon but the windows are black. Mandy is lying half out of her mummy bag. Her eyelids are large smooth bulges; they catch light as does the ridge of her skinny left shoulder. Martha steps over her and tries to see past the glass. They are high up, perhaps on the top floor. Martha rubs the window with her sleeve, squints, and gets an eyeful of night. She makes out sloping layered planes, like bird wings. Rooftops. Above and behind two candleless prickets, less black than the night into which they poke their priestly spikes, seven yellow stars are countable.

In Concord Martha saw the night from the ground; here she feels she is in it, in a pendant black cave. She wants out, down. She wants to dig her husband's grave.

She dresses in her new coat and boots and takes the elevator. Beneath his shelf of keys, the night clerk is asleep. She is out, on snow and cobblestone. Under a streetlamp she passes a woman in fur over pink boots. She says *good evening*; the woman says *hau ab*.

Ramistrasse. Heirschengraben. A bushy charcoal cat walks with her. The animal is at home. These are its streets. Limmat-Quai. A tight family of gulls make belly-sounds on a balustrade. The night lifts or is pushed on. Colour returns to the world. The river is no longer an ebony bone. It flickers. The buildings turn grey, grey-brown, green, pale pink, yellow, ashen, rust. Martha has made a circle. She walks past Bellevueplatz and picks up a path along the lake. She crosses a man with a dog. He says *guten morgen* and she *good morning* though she isn't sure time is going backwards. She enters a park with a giant object in a clearing. It is a dormant metal machine with gears, pulleys, cranks, shafts, spinning-wheels, weights, hinges, rollers, and coils. It is laced with snow. As Martha steps forward the machine bursts to life. First cause, second cause, third cause to where all the parts are moving.

Tinguely cockadoodles.

Beyond Martha and the machine the sky turns an icy blue.

*

Clad in her uniform of patched jeans and thick sweater, Mandy was sitting on the bed puffing on a messy cigarette. Her eyes were jaded, her wire-rims tucked back in her hair.

"Where the hell ya been, Granny?"

"I woke up and couldn't sleep so I went out for a walk."

"I dunno bout you, but I feel like I'm in the twilight zone."

Martha, now a bit more hip, told her it was probably the rabbit pellets and the funny cigarette.

"Honey, here it's seven in the morning. Back home it's eleven at night and here's the two of us just woke up from beddy-bye. I ain't quite figured it out yet, but I bet if they threw monkeys in those jets, they'd have some blown-out primates on their hands once they got 'em here." She puffed at the dying combustible.

"It's different here, Mandy, but it's pretty. I must have walked two miles. I don't think I've done that since Ray."

"Ray your dog?"

"He was my husband."

"Oh. Listen, don't go off leavin' like that without tellin' little Mandy where you're cartin' your ass."

"It was thirty years ago."

"Your dog?"

"My husband."

"You have a husband?" Between joint and jet lag Mandy's mind was blurred. Martha didn't care, however, because other than the clerk downstairs, Mandy was the only person in the new world who spoke to her in English.

"I had one thirty years ago."

"Oh…Ya hungry? I'm starved."

"For somebody as thin as you, Mandy, you sure eat a lot."

"Eatin's breathin', baby. Mama used to say I'd eat three bowls of pabulum and the shit don't even taste good. I remember she'd take me over to the Tropicana cause kids were 49 cents all-you-could-eat, or summin' like that, and I'd put away two plates of desserts before we started eatin'."

"Well, consider yourself one of the chosen – if I eat a handful of jujus they show up the next day on my résumé."

Since meeting Mandy, Martha found herself speaking more like a good churchgoer than Martha-the-Concorder. She was politer and cleaner. Proof, perhaps, of some subtle inter-human ongoing dialectic. With the Elroys she let her craps, pisses, asses, bitches and exclamation points run free (true, with Joan she held back a little). With Mandy on the other end, she let the girl-woman do the dirty talking for her. And Mandy – since she had squirmed into adolescence – was one to heave more and more shit as the walls got whiter.

For breakfast they were served café au lait and two croissants downstairs in the little hotel cafeteria.

"From the airport to here, I don't think I've seen a fat person. Have you?"

"Just you."

"These pigeon-meals might get me back into my wedding gown."

Martha called the waiter who grabbed a basket of croissants from a neighbouring table and laid it in front of her. Her stomach pleaded for bacon and eggs and toast and jam and hash browns. This she conveyed to the waiter who smiled, retreated to the kitchen and took a deep drag on his cigarette.

"Listen, like I think I better hit Amsterdam."

"Uh huh."

"If I don't catch my friends now I ain't gonna catchum, so maybe we can like set up a rendezvous at Snow White's Castle or the Matterhorn or summin and do our thing together later on?"

"Sure."

"That's what we used to do when the ol'man took me and Mama down to Dizzyland."

"Okay."

"Tell ya what. I'll call the hotel here in three days and you call 'em first and tell 'em exactly where you'll be in say a week's time and then if everythin's cool with Juliette and the rest of the crew we'll meet up where you say. How's that?"

"Sure Mandy."

Martha saw herself waiting for three hours at the bus station in Del Mar, smelling saltwater, then seeing the glow on the soldier's chest turn from star to cross as he approached with the news of a life shattered.

They both wrote down the phone number of the Hotel Otter and taxied to the Bahnhof. It was a Saturday morning and the station was full of soldiers in pine green uniforms carrying rifles that looked heavy and good for killing.

Mandy's train was at 10:37 so she was the first to go. At 11:04 Martha climbed into the red restaurant car of an Inter-City that was headed south. Minus Mandy, a train ride seemed better than a frozen town, and a ride in a restaurant better still.

The dining car was full. Martha dropped her suitcase in the aisle and made it a stool. As the train moved out a pleasant balding waiter asked Martha to decamp. German, French, and Italian had no effect, but when he tried to move her on in English Martha said, "Listen schmuck, my kingdom for a burger."

Good fortune had it that she had fallen on a gentleman. He lifted her arm and escorted her to a table at the rear of the wagon where he sat in moments of lull. He put her suitcase on the overhead rack, brushed crumbs from the white tablecloth, and handed her a menu with coloured pictures of wine, cheese, ravioli, steak, salad, and a plate of émincé zurichoise and hash browns. Howling deprived digestive hole made her pupils flicker and loneliness flee. Ordering by pointing, Martha rubbed her index into the émincé, potatoes, salad, and cheese.

By Aarau she wanted more rösti; when the blue signs of Olten flew past her window she was out of émincé and Emmental; and by the time the ticket collector confronted her shortly before Bern, she had fully dined twice.

Up against two plates of tasty food the world outside got little of Martha's attention. The snow-covered sun-drenched flat land west of Zurich escaped her entirely, and as they turned south bringing the Jura and a few hilltop castles into view, Martha was shovelling salad voraciously and grinding the leaves between her remaining silver-capped teeth. After Solothurn she was glancing out at the forest and scattered farms, but the waiter put an end to it when he delivered an unexpected bowl of chocolate mousse.

Bern would have been Martha's temporary home, but the 404 Inter-City drew away from the capital before Martha could pay her bill and put on her parka.

She left the restaurant car and went to a compartment with eight green seats. Her arrival was not undetected because, in lowering herself into the free seat, she let loose a muffled tube of wine and mustard sauce gas. She excused herself smiling.

Martha scouted the compartment for a potential friend. Across sat a young couple reading pamphlets about Morocco. Next to them was a woman about forty-five with tightly drawn lips that turned down at the corners where they intersected creases dropping to the point of her chin. She was reading a newspaper called *Der Bund* which she lowered from time to time revealing a yellow golf shirt with an alligator on it. Martha thought if she played golf she probably didn't have much fun. (What makes soft rounded lips of youth wither and fade like rotten shrimp? Golf? *Der Bund?* Der alligator shirt? At 30 parallel slits appear in the centre of the forehead above the nose bone; at 40 the skin under the lower lip relaxes and puffs at the edges; at 50 the lips are pulled back and in as though tongue and teeth are crying for company; at 70 the portrait is done, lips vanished, leaving the face a seeing, baked, cracked cube of desert mud. *Der Was?*)

The other four seats were occupied by sleeping soldiers, the sight of whom made Martha wonder if there wasn't a war. She had seen no dead.

She offered jujus as tokens of peace, and maybe more, to all who weren't sawing logs. After a quick shake of the head, the woman with the reptile on her shirt drew her lips to a point and ground her molars. The young couple refused with whispered *nein dankes.* Martha ate all the yellow and green ones, putting only a few reds in savings.

The train plunged and curved through a hillside of vines held high by rusted metal stakes. Out the left window Martha alone gaped at a huge grey-green lake sewn to a chain of towering white mountains. At track 1 in Lausanne all got out excepting the weary-eyed military quartet.

*

April 8, 1974

Dear Mom and Dad and Family,

I just got a second cause I put Bradley in the bathtub with his twenty-seven plastic fish, frogs, subs, etc. and Jerry took Andy and Richelle to the Arctic Circle for dinner. Better a tiny letter than no letter!

The week's been helterie skelterie starting with Monday in the middle of the night when Andy wakes up coughing like a dying cow and he's got the croop again. I rushed him in the bathroom and turned on the sink and tub hot water steamin and tried to calm him cause he was pretty nervous not being able to breathe and all. I was up for an hour and finally got him breathing ok – actually if it wasn't for all the paint falling off the bathroom ceiling it wouldn't be so bad. At least now we know what to do.

On Tuesday he was back in school so I got a call from Clixie and we went to MacFarline's Pie for lunch. We kinda just had dessert and no lunch cause we both felt we deserved it cause her husband's in Wendover for some kind of coupon convention or whatever and her youngest just got out of the hospital last week with a blocked colon. I had banana cream and then a yummy piece of apricot cheesecake. YYIPPes! Bradley's floodin the bathroom!

Later… Well so much for r and r. Bradley had thrown all his toys on the floor with half the ocean so there went ten of my letterwriting minutes down the drain. Jerry'll be back any second so I'll just tell you about Relief Society yesterday since it was a fantastic lesson about following the Lord even in times of Darkness and Doubt. Sister Swansen gave the example of a pilot flying through thick black clouds and who follows this little beep on his radar. She said we're all pilots and the Lord is this still small beep and if we follow it to the T we'll all find Him to the Celestial Kingdom. I thought it was pretty neat anyway so I wanted to pass it along.

Ding dong! Kids are home with Jerry. Please send the letter on to Aunt Martha. I'll write soon. Hope Bradley hasn't drowned.

Love Amber

Elroy passed the letter to his wife who was lunching on cottage cheese and sliced pineapple while watching *As The World Turns*. At the half time commercials she read it then put it in her apron pocket.

Before going to the mailbox, Elroy had been trying to think up or out an invention. His big ideas (*THE BIG EDGE* and the *CHILL-Y-OUT* tub) had come while doing something related. Other lesser creations were revealed when he lay alone in the living room listening to Anna Moffo records. (The rubber tomato slicer came in the second act of *La Bohème*. As the cantatrice streamed through Cherubino's "Non so più" from *Figaro*, birth was given to a triangular mirrored birdcage to help canaries fight solitude.)

After his daughter's letter he went back to the couch, but the sole newness his mind produced was a series of images in which sister Martha was entangled. Moffo sang "Misera, dove son?" and Martha was chucking icicle-spears at skiers from a chalet balcony. During the *Great Mass in C minor* she was throwing gobs of fondue at her TV because the machine refused to speak English, and in the third syllable of the *Hallelujah*, Martha, famished and penniless, was chasing a squealing pig across a bridge in Lucerne. The record stopped and his next of kin was dangling dead in an abandoned chair lift, a hungry alpine crow pecking at her skull as it unfroze with spring's arrival.

*

In fact, she lay on a bed in the Hotel AlaGare wondering why she had come.

Leaving was easy. The portrait of the Duchess, the postcards on the refrigerator, and her imagination told her there was another world. Elroy got her to the airport, the plane did the rest. Her petunias and petticoat narcissi would live without her. Mrs. Ruffenacht would see to that. Elroy cared she lived, she knew, but where did not matter. She had adopted a mutt that had licked her neck and tail-wagged her ankles until it splattered midway across the freeway, but other than that her body had had no receivers. A house doesn't miss you, does it? Or a TV?

She opened her suitcase and unrolled the Duchess. She laid her on the bed using shoes on the corners to keep her flat. *Why am I here?* Martha asked.

La Duchesse, hand round like a baby's, rose and lifted the water jug, letting three clear drops fall on Martha's head.

> *In the name of the Father, the Son, and the Holy Ghost*
> *I thee consecrate, I thee wed*
> *having gone this far we go on forever*
> *so it be*
> *the flesh and flowers one*
> *anointed, appointed, the Lord's bouquet*
> *His creations never azygous*
> *thee and I between His fingers molded held in His hands*
> *over, under, and in amen*

Martha turned Her face to the mirror to study the gift being given. Placing her own picture on the headboard, the Duchess positioned herself on the pillows behind Her and began stroking Her hair with cherubic fingers, unravelling the auburn matt. She then cupped her hands over Her sagged uneven eyes and glided the fingertips round and round and back as if she were levelling sand. She slid her hands past the curve of Her nostrils and kneaded gently and long the sunken skin outside Her jaw. With her thumbs and forefingers she pulled and raised the threefold chin until Her face was all heat.

In the rectangular pine-framed mirror Martha watched the Duchess sculpt. What Jean-Marc Nattier did to her, she did to Martha – though the medium was not paint but pulpy aged avoirdupois – twenty and two hundred years later.

Her shoulders were trimmed, Her neck halved, Her breasts packed tight like hamburger patties. The apricot cardigan fell to Her waist and white chiffon was laid low-cut baring Her chest and upper arms. The Duchess left untouched the chestnut eyes, but scraped away the bulging lids and with pinched fingers drew two finely curved brows. Linear purity replaced the feminine version of the Elroy crooked snout, then the cheekbones were raised and angled flowing to a mouth that was made to look like a bidden fruit.

Martha watched the Duchess place a string of petunias round Her shoulder and down Her front, then slide the water jug into what was visible of Her right hand.

They were One in a slowly darkening room. There was a soft knock at the door, it cracked open letting in first Hiller's hand. The floor groaned as he stealthily moved to the bed. She sensed him, emitting a vague odour of fish that he recognised at once. They fell locked in embrace into a heap on the bed, but when She made for his blood-filled cane it burst bloodying what it could.

He had wanted her.

*

The Rue de Simplon isn't much wider than a basketball player's wingspan. When you get off a train in Lausanne you can exit north or south. Martha had gone south because it was downhill. She had arrived in late afternoon, passed through a tunnel under the tracks, and fought with her valise down twenty-odd steps. Trains halted overhead in squealing crescendo.

She looked left into a sooty alley, ahead at a cracker-box audio shop whose wares were displayed behind wire mesh (do the thieves work before or after they use the train?), then stepped through a urine-stained corridor to the Rue de Simplon. Fifty metres east, the Hotel AlaGare beckons the weary traveller.

I had followed Martha off the train and watched her, bowlegged hunch under an oversized parka, plod along the sidewalk to the hotel. Getting off the train she had said, "Somebody turn on the son-a-bitchin' heat," to no one in particular. She spoke my language and was going my way.

The sight of this woman – assuredly American – stayed with me because looking wholly out of place, she seemed in place.

I was reminded of a scene I'd witnessed in Venice the spring before. Drinking a mid-morning espresso and grappa in a bar on the Rio de Maddalena, my eyes fell on a black mound. I was standing at the counter and had been squinting to read the labels on the upside-down bottles behind the bartender who was reading the *Gazzetta dello Sport*. We had both failed to see her come in. She was sixty or seventy, dressed in black wool. Her skull sprouted sparse ashy hair that looked unwashed since her husband's death, whenever that was. In one hand she held a nylon shopping bag full of green vegetables and jonquils. In the other her bony fingers clutched a 500-lire note and were close to losing a fight with gravity over some eels that were squirming out of a brown paper wrapper. She too wanted coffee. She looked up at me and smiled, all four feet of her. I stood with elbows on a counter that was built for people who, when seated on a kitchen chair, have legs long enough to reach the floor. She stood under the counter out of the bartender's view. She waited patiently for three or four minutes, threw me a toothless grin, did an about-face and left.

I had a second grappa and hated myself for not helping.

A third and I hated all creation.

I gulped a fourth and went out in Venice's ethereal light.

Joy almost killed me.

When I trailed Martha I felt a similar passion. She looked utterly lost, in need, but, like the midget wanting coffee after the mercato, singularly right about being where she was. This time I knew why I didn't intervene, but only watched Martha's hike from train to hotel. Divinity is not to be fooled with, but I guess it needs a witness.

I saw Martha Hiller three other times in the neighbourhood. Once on a gorgeous Sunday morning in May she was throwing handfuls of dried bread to swans and honking gulls in Ouchy. I observed her for a dozen minutes and never did she gape at the grand Alps across the lake. She showed no sign of being a tourist and, when her paper bag was empty, she tossed it in the water.

The second encounter was a few days later in the Migros MM grocery store down the street from her hotel. She pulled up behind me in line at the check stand holding a litre of chocolate ice cream and a basket of early Spanish strawberries. I felt her staring at the right half of my face until she elbowed me in the chops and said, "I'll be a flat-tired motorcycle! If it isn't James Dean!" She began calling other people in line to meet me before jumping in my arms to give me a wet smooch. I feigned linguistic ignorance and tried to calm her down. True, I had a nose like the dead star, but other than that I could think of nothing that could have brought her lips to mine.

My son was the reason for my last sighting of her. My wife was out and I was working next to the ironing board in my cluttered study. Gerald had recently learned to fold paper airplanes and was launching a fresh white fleet from our streetside balcony. One hit Martha's ear *(c'était droit dans l'oreille PoPi!)* as she was passing by. I heard a blast of sound that was between laughter and shriek. I ran to the balcony and there she was trying to play catch with my son with his cock-eyed planes.

When the local newspaper reported her death, they – with typical Swiss discretion – mentioned no name. "An American tourist" was all they said. The morgue in Lausanne wouldn't let me see her, and when I got to Bern she was already crumbs.

*

Mandy, Juliette, *et al.* were doing Europe and undoing the buttons on their jeans. The sixties it was, and though most of it was bluff, sometimes the flower goddesses really did go down on the grass or under the glow of a vanilla moon. Dope was usually the helpful cantharis, or – in Mandy's case – the great equalizer. When she was high and her glasses fogged, a Dutchman was a Dane was a German was a Parisian was a Florentine. From country to country, city to city, the moon and the men shed the same pale flicker. Jorg was Georg was Georges was Giorgio. The moment was a half-filled glass, and when a guy named Jorge had shot his wad into Mandy's gelatinous ocean, he fell, like a raindrop on the North Sea, quickly into obscurity.

Juliette had recovered from high school and her good looks helped the group save on hotel and hostel bills. Men usually found them before fatigue did. In the north the indigenes always had beds; in the south they knew where the ground was softest.

Mandy should have called the Hotel Otter from Copenhagen. But the memory is a sieve and sometimes chunks even as big as Martha slip through the mesh. One life subtracted from another.

Four weeks and fourteen cities later, Mandy was back to Jocko with a small bag of old new tricks. Juliette, her backpack exchanged for Italian leather, said she was on her way to Hollywood.

*

The franc was almost four to a dollar. Martha struck a deal with the manager of the Hotel AlaGare: twenty francs a day, sheets changed every second Monday, no breakfast, no maid service, and no TV. She paid May in advance, and told Monsieur Gay-Lussac that if the swans were still hungry she'd stay through July.

April had been inordinately sunny. The snow that had been dumped on Martha's arrival seemed to have drained the sky. Sometimes a few thin clouds hung like halos over the tips of the Alps. Mostly the days were blue. Day by day, inch by inch, the white skirt that bound the mountains rose until the snow held only in the high shaded crooks. The lawn in the park by the lake grew greener; red and yellow tulips started pulling out of their bulbs.

Martha wandered the lakeside every day. She was usually awake by eight, in her paisley dress and apricot sweater by half past, and in a pastry shop at a quarter to nine. She would buy a bagful of boules de Berlin or *les cornets à la vanille* for herself and beg for any leftovers for the birds. *Oiseau* was the first French word she learned. "For da wahzohs," she'd say. Three hundred yards down the Avenue d'Ouchy and her babies came squawking.

Most of the birds had stopped migrating decades ago. Their feathers had thickened and their blood had cooled. Christmases were spent in nests fashioned in lakeside nooks. Daytime January to March they glided through the steel water near the shore hunting a hand with a sack of dried bread. Donors were cooed until the crusts and crumbs started flying, then it was war, one against all.

With jackhammer beak and quick wings, a gull can rip a morsel from the grasp of a duck, moorhen, or swan. Once it's got it, it rises like a helicopter and flees the mob. Anything thrown upward is snatched at its zenith. The gulls eat the most and make the most noise. Periodically, as if given some heavenly signal, they all take flight and leave the other birds a moment to lunch in relative peace.

The swans peck the ducks and moorhens to create space. With their rubber necks they gobble what falls within a three-foot radius. When the feeder crushes a dry half loaf on the asphalt, the sparrows scurry in and pounce on the leftover beige dust. Slow, passive, dumb, the moorhens are born losers. They act as if they don't mind. They seem to go for food not out of conviction but in imitation of the howling brutes around them. Can survival be an act or mimicry?

Martha distributed her rations as equitably as she could. Sometimes she pretended her bag was empty, waited for the dominant fowls to disappear, then snuck a few bits to the weaklings. Or she'd throw wide left and wide right to distract the gulls, then hurriedly heave a few handfuls to the moorhens that unwittingly hadn't gone for the fakes.

As the weather got warmer and the food more plentiful, Martha fed the birds quickly and took to strolling toward Pully. On the narrow ledge above the lake she rubbed shoulders with spring's first lovers. Schools of baby perch dawdled in their newly granted world. Minnows darted like sparks below Martha's heavy brown shoes. Boats with yellow, white, and baby-blue sails walked on the water as ghosts in an empty house.

In her early outings sight was not the most active of Martha's senses. Sounds and smells were more prominent: the engines of foreign cars on neighbouring roads, water licking itself at the shore, the raucous hungry birds, air thicker than in Concord sticking to her nostrils in morning or early evening, whiffs of swan dung rising from nesting areas, the algal odour of a living lake.

In a sense, Martha was relearning to walk. At home she had walked to the bus stop and through a shopping mall or a grocery store. Here, as a child, she was walking just to walk.

*

Bradley is in his crib. His mother in her bed. The other kids are at school. Jerry is looking at property.

He awakes, stares at his corduroy frog, says *Bock, bock.* He stands gazing past the bed rail. He lifts one leg and straddles the bar. His diaper is soaked so when it presses against the wood, urine runs down his bare skin. He climbs out. This is the first time he has done so. He turned two last week.

The room is dim, but Bradley knows it well. He reaches back in for his frog and pulls it through the bars. He thump-walks to the door saying *Mamo, bock.* He opens the door, but back-pedals into his room for his rag. He thump-walks to the hall, wipes his eyes. He goes to the bathroom and in a muffled whine says *Wa, mamo, wa.* He climbs on a miniature chair and throws the contents of a tooth care glass on the floor. He fills the glass with water, drinks three gulps, then drops the rest on the pink tile.

He unrolls ten feet of toilet paper forgetting to wipe his leg. He turns on the light as he goes out.

Afternoon sun beckons him to the living room. Bradley pulls Bible, Book of Mormon, Doctrine and Covenants, and Reader's Digest off coffeeless coffee table. He rips out Second Corinthians, half of Moroni, and advice on how to buy retreaded tires. Recovers rag and frog thump-walks to cork-like pebbles at the base of potted tree. Pebbles thrown, Bradley's fingers flap.

Recovers rag and frog and thump-walks to kitchen. Climbs on chair at table, grabs pen with tightened fists, scribbles on plastic tablecloth. Rubs loose ink with pinkies and thumbs. Recovers rag and frog and in descending pulls tablecloth. Toaster and spice shakers collide with Freshco Fuchsia linoleum floor from Montgomery Ward's.

Mother wakes. Recovers Bradley. *Oh my stars you little dickens you.*

Mo wa, mamo.

*

Neither he nor his horse had moved for fifteen years. Martha wanted to sit behind him interlocking her fingers on the belly-button button of his military coat and squeeze. It was not hero worship because she knew nothing of how he had masterfully readied for world war a trilingual army.

They had met on the sixth of May, Martha's birthday, though neither cared what day it was. Martha was cutting across a gravel path between the Beau Rivage Hotel and the lake with a bag of stale croissants. She was listening to her darling's call when she tripped. Tumbling, she cursed fecal matter and looked up at the General perched on his steed. Neck erect under a brimmed hat, eyes brass balls, he remained poised in the face of Martha's invectives. He held the reins firmly, his gloved hand an instant from his pistol.

Martha got up and dusted the purple paisley near the thighs. She glanced up at the General. Her body quivered. Was what she had felt for Ray Hiller that was back again? Was it the uniform? She swallowed the lump in her throat, her face reddened. After picking up her bag of croissants, she told the General she'd be back the next day and crossed the street to the lake.

Knowing when and where you can see someone can be a comfort. At sundown, when walking back home, Martha purposely stayed on the lakeside of the street. She threw the General a cursory glance but maintained her highest possible bosom for a good two hundred yards.

That evening she broke the habit of eating in her room and dined downstairs in the Restaurant Le Raccard. She wore her grey suit and was greeted by Monsieur Gay-Lussac who escorted her to a corner table and recommended she try a plate of raclette.

"Madame must taste our speciality. Our cheese is ze finest from ze Valais."

Martha said sure.

"And what vould you drink vith it?"

"Just gimme a coke."

"But Madame viz a Coca-Cola you destruct ze taste of ze cheese and you have problems viz ze stomach."

"Wha d'ya suggest, Gay?" She assumed Gay was his first name.

"You must have a vite vine viz it." Martha had no idea what a "vite vine" was but gave the green light.

The waiter first brought a tiny glass and a small pitcher of an almost yellow liquid. He filled the glass which Martha downed in two healthy gulps. He refilled… and he re-refilled.

Next came a dish with small pickles and onions. Martha ate most of them immediately and found they complimented the wine which was already leaking to her brain.

Gay-Lussac brought the first portion of raclette. She gawked at the little gob of melted cheese and the dwarf potato and made a seagull sound.

"But you can have as much as you vant," he said to assure her.

"In that case," Martha said, "Let's get started."

She ate seven portions and was served another carafe of the vite vine. She had been drunk once before in her life, the evening prior to her husband's departure to Camp Pendleton. She wondered then if she had sinned, but the night had felt wonderfully warm and life had presented so few sinful occasions that she decided God wouldn't mind either way.

The waiter paid and generously tipped (she still didn't quite understand all the money), she staggered upstairs to her room. As she drifted into sleep in her paisley gown, the mirror, the curtains, and the Duchess circled the bed like watchful hawks.

She was up and in Ouchy before the streetlamps turned off. The cars were coated with a thin dew; it felt like Easter morning.

The horse's slippery metal leg was longer than she had remembered. Clinging to the General's gun she hoisted herself a couple of inches and was able to plant her right shoe on a hind kneecap. With one solid thrust she swung her leg over the animal's rump and hugged for dear life the General's manly waist. She settled herself rubbing her pelvis into his chilly coccyx. She swallowed a breath of Guisan's bedewed bronzy scent. She looked where he looked – into the heart of a sycamore tree.

A policeman brought the tryst to an early end. Finding communication impossible (all Martha said was "wahzoh"), he helped her down from the statue and thought it best to release her to her mother earth.

*

Rarely did she venture into the upper parts of Lausanne. One warm day in June she took the tunnel back through the station and hiked up the cobblestones to Place St. François. It was nine-thirty and pigeons outnumbered shoppers. She walked around the stone church then up between the stores on the Rue de Bourg, pausing to watch a silent TV through the window of an audio-visual shop. A sudden thundershower sent her back downhill.

She never got up to the Riponne, the cathedral, or the animal park in Sauvablin. (She had enough to feed at the lake.) Nor did she see the Roman ruins in the Vidy park. Geneva was avoided because she didn't know it was there.

It had been much the same in Concord. A shuttle bus took her to the Sun Valley Mall where she could find everything she needed, except gardening equipment and groceries. For these she had Mrs. Ruffenacht and Mrs. Ruffenacht's Dodge, twice weekly, for a jaunt to the Park 'N Shop. Otherwise she kept to her home on Willow Pass Road. Once in a while, Elroy took her for a drive through Golden Gate Park and the Japanese Tea Gardens, but beyond that San Francisco was a foreign city. After Ray died she spent a couple of months in a mind clinic in Napa. The attending doctors, to their credit, quickly decided she could likely as not do life without them. When her dog was killed she had another downswing and told Mrs. Ruffenacht she was going to run across the highway until they got her too. Her neighbour kept her in sight until Elroy arrived. He set her up with a friend, a Mormon psychotherapist, who visited her Monday mornings. He would come after *The Lucy*

Show and they, Martha and counsellor, spent most of their time discussing Lucy and Desi's chances of making the Celestial Kingdom. Did Lucy smoke? Did God care? Was Desi the fornicating type? Did they drink Maxwell House? Would the decaffeinated kind close the pearl gates?

The counsellor tried to bring the concepts of love and self-esteem into Martha's Weltanschauung, but at the time she was more concerned with the Arnez's salvation than her own wellbeing.

The psychotherapist kept up his visits until he thought Martha was no longer a danger to herself. Fifteen weeks had been enough. Elroy tried to pay him but he refused, saying he knew Elroy would have done the same.

With big blanks between their meetings Elroy often imagined his sister's life. As far back as their childhood in Oakland, he recalled trying to fill in the gaps between point A and point B. She was in high school, he in junior high. They would part ways after breakfast and meet again for dinner. He would ask what she'd done and she'd say *not much* or *Mom, is there any dessert?* When she got a D in chemistry he wondered what had gone wrong between her and the molecules. Once he found her sobbing and drooling into her pillow. He knew she was heartbroken, but by whom and under what circumstances stayed frozen in her tears. When she brought Ray Hiller home for Thanksgiving, Elroy divined they had met in MacTavish's Ice Cream Parlor where she had had a summer job. Not long after Elroy was living in Baltimore.

Europe was the widest gorge and forever would be. Cinders can't talk. Martha probably wouldn't have anyway. He couldn't help wondering, had they been spatially closer, would it have really made a difference?

*

The road nearest the lake from Lausanne to Pully is named after General Guisan. Martha wasn't the only one to be impressed. It's a straight shot for about three quarters of a mile with a sidewalk on the south side. Between the street and Lac Leman, the rich hide themselves in mansions surrounded by high walls and shrubby fences. Like Martha, most pedestrians take the path beside the water.

She fed the birds in the small cove at the entrance of the walkway just past the Tour Haldimand. They ate less; it was August and about as hot as it gets in Switzerland. Dropping the paper bag she chanted

"Adieu wahzoo adieu". Her French vocabulary was now eight words: *bonjour, un, deux, trois, ça, coco* (slang for horse – or horsie – that she picked up playing with children in the Denantou Park), *adieu* and *oiseau.* Given she'd never understand when asked a yes-no question, *oui* and *non* hadn't stuck.

The air was heavy, full of annoying gnats. A glaze from the summer heat hung over the lake making the mountains across the water look like heaps of soiled chiffon. Swimmers dove from stalled sailboats. Shirtless men oared women and children in shiny lacquered rowboats. Few Swiss walk when the temperature rises past eighty-five; they have ten other months to make their bodies warm.

Beneath her skirt with the arched palm trees, Martha's thighs stuck. She wore her light brown blouse; damp half-moons swung from her armpits. She carried flat shoes, using them periodically to beat at the bugs. Bits of golden gravel lodged between her toes and in the corrugations on the bottom of her feet.

In spite of its inconveniences, Martha welcomed the heat. A body used to something lets the thing in more easily than a body with other habits. Concord summers had often been in the hundreds, and in Sacramento you could have fried your pancakes on the blacktop.

She walked on.

In some places there were sandy spots with scattered sunbathers, in others huge granite boulders reinforced the shoreline.

At a tad after two Martha was in the Parc de Pully. She found a seat on a bench under a fanning elm. Hearing the sparrows chatter, she wished she had saved some bread. Kids teeter-tottered, swooped down slides, bucked on wooden mounts, and hooted at their parents what Martha took to be cries of hunger and thirst. At a small stand she bought a thick sausage on a slice of bread and cardboard plate with a mustard mound for dipping. The meat she ate, the rest she broke for friends hopping at her feet.

On her walks, rare was the person who addressed her. When it happened she smiled and said *bonjour* with such a hard "j" that she gave away both her nationality and language ignorance with a single word. This day was another mute one, but it didn't matter. The Swiss are good people but not known for their loquacity.

She went on to the port where the boats stood motionless, tied to the dock like tired horses. A few skippers in skimpy bathing suits washed their hulls and fiddled with chords. There was no going out in the dead air.

She turned and looked up the hill behind her at a homey angular church perched atop a sloping vineyard. She wanted a moment out of the heat and why not share it with her Saviour?

A high rock wall had been built between the vines and the steep passage up to the church. Mid-route Martha braced herself against it and rested her lungs. She came to a cluster of old narrow houses that had recently been converted into beauty salon, pharmacy, tobacco outlet, clothes boutique, shoe repair shop, electrical shop, gallery, pastry distributor, and the quaint village café. Like Martha once said, "The old was once new and the new will be old, so don't sweat it either way."

The church sat on a round plateau. Martha stood at the carved door panting, perspiration oozing from her mahogany crown. She went in and took a seat at the rear right pew. Alone, she, amid the elegant Gothic curves.

> *Our Father who art in heaven*
> *Hallowed by Thy name*
> *Thy Kingdom come*
> *Thy will be done*
> *In earth as it is in heaven.*

As she cooled, the words rose to the surface, up from age eight. And the bread had been given, the debtors forgiven, temptation rotten for years.

The church smelt like a dank ditch.
In the name of the father
fled and dead
The son
child never made
And the holiest of ghosts
you, dear Martha, you
Amen

The four o'clock sun poured through the stained glass.

Martha looked at Jesus but saw Hiller then Elroy then Hiller. Her back was cold so she leaned forward. The air was no warmer than the wood. She heard her brain buzz but it wasn't her brain but a wasp that had followed her in. It buzzed louder and lit on the base of her neck driving its stinger into her sweet skin. Martha slapped it senseless.

Woozy, she got up and left by the south side door. She found herself in a gravel garden with shaded benches set equidistant between a line of plane trees. In front, a low stone barrier protected passers-by from the vineyard below. Martha dragged herself to a bench and lay down. She and the pain in her neck went to sleep.

Her hand went up.

"Sister Swansen, what happens if an itsy-witsy baby

dies?"

Did you lose a loved one Martha?

"No ma'am, but if a baby dies does it get to go to heaven?"

The Lord takes care of His children when they don't get a fair chance to prove their righteousness.

"When's a baby not a baby no more?"

The yellow jacket revived. Its right side wouldn't move. Half its wings were wrinkled like crushed cellophane. Three of its legs were powder. The good wings quivered. It slid sideways on its belly to the edge of the bench and fell to the floor.

Well dear, you were baptized at eight because the Lord has told us that this is the age when we can decide wrong from right.

"But what if your brain buzzes and you feel like you're on one of them Tilt-a-Whirls they got at the carnival?"

What do you mean Martha?

"I mean – well – not necessarily me – but what if somebody don't have a brain that fits right in the head and makes funny sounds?"

You mean the mentally handicapped?

"Yeah, somethin' like that."

The Lord passes no judgment on these people and they are delivered directly into His hands.

"Thank you, Sister Swansen."

It moved two more feet and settled into a crack in the cold stone floor under the last pew. It was brain-dead when Martha awoke. Its antennae and left wing fluttered at irregular intervals. The black spots vibrated on the yolk-coloured back.

The sky was an orangish pink. The haze on the lake had thinned as the day grew cooler. Martha sat up and scratched the lump under her hair. She put on her shoes. Feeling light she half tiptoed to the wall to play tightrope.

"Is it okay Sister Swansen?"

Silence was *yes* so she raised her skirt and climbed up. The wall wasn't much more than knee-high, on top as wide as a book though slightly rounded. She rose to full height spreading her arms and fingers as if holding the air for support. She advanced one, two, three, four little steps.

"Look at me Sister Swansen – I'm in the circus!" she said turning her head left toward the lake. Just before she fell she saw, for an instant, sky, mountains and water as a singular salmon slab.

Though the drop was only seven or eight feet her extra weight sent the rusty iron stake clean through her. It severed the portal vein, the cystic duct, and the hepatic artery as it shot through the side of her stomach. She bled blood and dark green bile on the mashed vine. A crow found her first, dancing on her back and pecking at her loose innards until the sky was filled with golden stars.

Mankind came at noon the next day.

*

The eighteenth fairway was barely visible as Elroy teed the ball. He made good contact and watched the tiny white sphere disappear in the purple blue. He thought he was somewhere down the middle. He picked up his bag and counted two hundred paces. From this point he crisscrossed the grass between the tall spectral eucalyptus. It had faded a bit but had hung on to the side of the fairway. He pulled out a seven iron and whacked the Titlist into the night. He tried but didn't see a thing.

In the clubhouse he had a beer then called Joan to see what was for dinner.

"I haven't started anything, honey, but I thought maybe we could barbecue."

"Call the Seamans and see if they've eaten."

"Okay dear. I'll start the fire."

"Be home in twenty minutes – oh, honey, we got any more of that corn on the cob?"

"Could be, if not I could run down to Safeway."

"I'll pick some up."

"I really think we've got a few ears."

"Ah right angel."

"How'd ya do?"

"Beheaded half the gophers."

"I'll get the charcoals going."

"Bye dear."

It was the Friday after the Labour Day. Elroy had played Tilden because evenings were cooler and less crowded than Walnut Creek. He had a forty-six on the front but stopped keeping score at thirteen after he sent two drives into the gully.

Bob and Carole Seaman walked down the hill. Crickets pounded the moonlit night. They had each been on their second Martini and had been unsure as to whether they'd go down to the Vintage House for chops or have pastrami on rye out by the pool. They were happy to get Joan's call. The coals were alive when they came through the back patio gate.

Moffo, on the 8-track, was breezing through "Com per me sereno…" from *La Sonnambula*. The Cadillac wound down the eastern Berkeley hills. Sometimes fog from the ocean rolled over in creamy waves. Tonight there was none. Elroy turned right on the Dam Road. His mind was nibbling at a new invention, or maybe it was the other way around. Recently it had been taking him a long time to get out of bed in the morning and he ventured this might be due to man's habit of sleeping flat. We spend the day perpendicular to the floor and suddenly we force the body parallel. Then, after the earth makes a third of a rotation, up it all goes again. In the headlights Elroy saw primates rising with the dawn in their caves and licking each other with long pink loving tongues. Since we made the mistake of standing up (hernias, backaches, crooked spines, slipped discs and the rest) let's at least learn to sleep right. In the mind's eye he saw an L-shaped bed in profile tilted back to about thirty degrees. He'd need to test the exact slope.

As he drove into the driveway he wasn't sure if he'd christen his creation the "Dream Sleeper" or "WakeUpRight".

They had rib-eye steaks, corn on the cob, garlic bread, and strawberry shortcake. Joan blessed the food and pretended not to look when her husband tore open a second six-pack of Budweiser.

When they were into dessert she told Elroy the county people had called again to know if they still hadn't received Mrs. Hiller's remains.

"So what did you say, honey?" Elroy asked.

"Well you know I can't really tell a lie, but a little white one now and then can't do too much harm, so I said she must have got lost in the mail."

"That's my girl."

Before going home Bob Seaman helped his friend carry a long patio bench to the bedroom. They put it in the corner against the wall, then hoisted the mattress and box springs into place making the first testing ground for man's journey into supreme slumber.

The Elroys made love in the bathroom then literally *climbed* into bed. Joan, after three slides under the sheets, slept down the hall in Amber's old bed. Elroy stuck out the night and when California turned toward the flaming sun, he awoke, bleary-eyed, in a heap on the floor.

Once the sin against God was the greatest sin; but God died, and these sinners died with him. To sin against the earth is now the most dreadful thing, and to esteem the entrails of the unknowable higher than the meaning of the earth.

Nietzsche
Thus Spoke Zarathustra

II

Neil Baker had stood behind the fence behind the hole that was just big enough to see everything and had felt like he did when he saw his father lay the tri-coloured ray gun under the Christmas tree. Then, far from sleep, he had crawled down the hall over the twine-like carpet into the living room and when he heard something coming, had slid surreptitiously behind the sofa. He saw his father drop the armful that had the ray gun he had supplicated – more than once – from the North Pole.

He felt then what he felt six years later standing behind the fence seeing Mr. Cantril blow a hole in the dog's head with the thirty-odd-six. A single solid sound had filled the neighbourhood for as far Neil Baker could hear, and it didn't stop sounding for minutes. The Cantril's dog's legs had crumpled like the branches of the Christmas tree when they put it to fire in the back yard. The branches had looked thin inside the flames like the dog's legs that had crumpled two at a time while the shot sound hung in Neil Baker's neighbourhood.

Behind the hole in the fence he had seen Mr. Cantril set the rifle on the ping-pong table and push-wiggle the dog into a black plastic bag, the kind for leaves. He saw him go into the garage with the bag knot above his thick knuckles. Then he couldn't see Mr. Cantril, but he heard the sound of the car trunk slam into the sound that filled the neighbourhood. Then the car drove off.

What Neil Baker felt, seeing from behind the sofa and behind the fence, was that behind his eyes there was a hole in his own head. There wasn't pain in his head, but when the hole dropped straight through his throat, and lodged just below his ribs, there was. The pain was dark purple. Some pains were brown-green, others were blue-black, but the ones Neil Baker got below the ribs were always the dark purple of rank meat.

Now he was standing over the grill with nothing going but a pair of chili-cheese burgers, feeling the bubble forming behind his brow. The Diner was dead. The Diner rush had been a dribble.

As nightfall encased Oakland, the streetlights on East 14th brought gnats into their halos and threw stripes onto the passing Pontiacs, Olses, and Chevys. It got darker out and lighter in. The canary yellow tube over Neil Baker's head could be seen a block away.

"Hey man – hold the onions on one em burgers," said the person on the other side of the oval aperture.

The asshole could have told me when he ordered, Neil Baker thought but didn't say. Then: *the muthafucker's probably eatin' both of them.* He slid the dead onions across the grill into the garbage slot-hole. He flipped the burgers and picked the two bottom buns off the grill. As he walked the three steps across the slats to the chili pot, the person said, "If it aint bustin your balls or nuttin, throw in a large order a dem crispy goldin Doggie Diner fries you done battized in last week's grease pool ova der."

Neil Baker dropped a ladleful of chili on each bun. Walking back to the grill he looked at the turquoise chartreuse orange knit cap tight like a swim bonnet on the person's head. He set the buns on the cool side of the grill, then bagged the fries. Looking back at the person's cap he said, "Ya takin this with ya?"

"You gawdit Jack."

"Ya drinkin summin' with that?"

"Gimme one a dem strawberry shakes you make with dem fresh rosy strawberries you got growing back der in da parkin lot."

Neil Baker took two steps to the shake machine. Hoping, trying, to keep the hole from dropping through his throat, he looked past the person's cap out onto East 14th. The gnats bouncing randomly in the light reminded him of mornings when Neil Baker the kid would sit up in bed next to the shaft of sun coming through the space between the curtains. In the light he would see the tiniest things jerking up, down, and across and he would think they were atoms. He would think he was seeing the smallest bits of the universe and that he, only he, could see them without a microscope. Every time the shaft of sunlight was there the atoms were there, and he would sit in his pyjamas, even when they were pee-wet and his feet not yet reaching the floor, and stare at what he thought only he could see.

"What's da damage gunna be?" the person asked pulling a handful of money from his trouser pocket.

Neil Baker was looking at the gnats.

"*Woo Ooouu!* Whad I owe you Jack?"

Neil Baker's eyes moved back to the person's cap. The person said, "Lissin man, it aint nunna my biness, but yor face look kina green like da moon up der on wunna dem good fuckin nights."

The hole was past the thorax, but Neil Baker said, "That's okay man. That'll be a dollar eighty-nine," as he scooped the person's coins off the counter. He watched the person's hand take the bag of food then move off down the sidewalk with the motion of a rocking cradle. Then he saw the imprinted pink lips on the back of the person's t-shirt that said **FREE**

THE PEOPLE. He imagined the front: a butthole saying **HOLD THE ONIONS**. But he had only seen the knit cap. Then he thought, give them – us – any more freedom and the zoo blows up.

He kicked open the swinging door to the back room and said, "Hey kid, watch the cage for a minute." He went out the back door to the john on the patio where he would try to vomit.

Aaron Elroy, eyes pink and moist from peeling, quartering, and chopping onions, straightened his Doggie Diner hat and entered the cage.

*

Cyndy Baker had been Cindy Talbot until they threw the rice. She had been the skinniest girl in the senior class at Las Lomas High which was one of the reasons Neil Baker married her. She was skinnier than he was. They wed four weeks to the day after the Senior All-Night. Saturday to Saturday to Saturday to Saturday had been enough to put the seeds of family in the pot. The first Saturday was spent rubbing, the second unbuttoning, the third unzipping, and the fourth naked but for sweat in the new Holiday Inn in Concord.

The family tree bore no fruit for the first five years of their marriage. Cyndy Baker deduced that you can't grow cherries on a toothpick. For five years she had pushed her cart through the aisle at Safeway past thousands of cut-off-clad fat ladies, their multiple offspring jostling and hanging from their chariots. Finally she went on an eating binge, prying wide her tummy with Oreos, Twinkies, burgers, dogs, shakes, sundaes and a heavy dose of carbohydrates. She would warm leftover spaghetti for breakfast or she'd ask Neil to bring her a Western Burger from the Diner that she'd have cold with her Cheerios. She kept a bag of chips an arm's length away.

Results were arithmetic at first, but by the seventh month her dress size started growing exponentially. After eleven months she was up to a sixteen and Bunny Blair Baker was in the basket. Dr. Wayson told her that her success had nothing to do with her waistline, but she was sure she knew better. Bunny came and, shortly after she stopped nursing, she was pregnant with Billy Nabisco whom she saw as a second living proof to her fertility theorem.

Cyndy never touched a drop of liquor until after Billy Nabisco was born. But with two of them to dress, wash, referee, and pick up after ("lak a gaddam street sweeper at a carnival") she took to having a couple of beers after the kids were in bed. Eventually two beers stopped being enough, so she had two beers and a slug of sour mash. As the children got older, fought more, and made bigger messes, she had her beers while they napped in the afternoon, then two slugs of whisky to replace the evening beers and another shot for the last shot. She was usually sloshed by ten thirty and would fall asleep on the couch with the TV tuned to the Channel 2 *Newswatch*. Her husband was home at two thirty to turn off the fuzz on the television screen. He would inevitably rise with Bunny and Billy at 7 am at which time she would lumber off the couch, curse life, and settle into the matrimonial bed. Neil Baker complained little about this schedule, not because he had had but one spouse and hence no comparative ground, but because he couldn't sleep much anyway.

After a year of watching his beloved thump from couch to bedroom leaving a trail of muffled invectives, he began to hate her. Again, this had nothing to do with his being over-worked. He hated her because as far as he could see she hated everything. She hated the laundry, the dishes, the furniture, the kids' crap, the house – her "gaddam scumbag life". When Baker tried to mount her on the couch after extinguishing the TV, he always hoped he would provide her with something not to be hated. The last time he had tried, she left him do it, then in the afterglow had said, "Next time use the keyhole."

She, he thought, also hated *him*.

As Neil Baker knelt dry heaving over the Doggie Diner toilet bowl, his wife's right hand was fingering an ounce of Old Crow on the kitchen table. She glared at the relics of dinner on the sink, stove, table and floor. She picked up the glass and walked out the back door to the lounge chair on the patio. The glow from the kitchen light cast a pale glimmer through the grass onto a sandbox and an overturned tricycle. She sank into the chair, poured the whisky down her throat, then lay down in the night like a horizontal pupa.

*

You enter the Doggie Diner from the sidewalk along East 14th or through the swinging doors from the parking lot in the rear. The patio is U-shaped, the U surrounding the cage and back room. A six-foot fence, the top foot windowed, separates the patio from the parking lot. If you dine at one of the turquoise Formica tables, you dine under a roof but in open air. You sit on a low blue stool that doesn't spin, and you are likely to leave your mess on the table rather than toss it in the garbage bin nearest you. Your chili stains and dried ketchup marks will come off. The fries you crush underfoot will be swept. You may pull a knife on your neighbour if he disturbs you or in some way brings your being to a boil. You'll probably be bluffing but you have been known to leave another's blood in the pores of the tile floor. This is harder to clean than spice drippings. On the other hand you may be gentle or meek, having chosen to carry your burdens rather than spill blood. You are likely poor, unless you're in the area on invitation to repair plumbing or estimate sewer damage. You are poor only in a manner of speaking, for you do dine, you have medicine, you have been vaccinated against polio and diphtheria, you sleep out of the cold, if you wish you can see things to call beautiful, and, given that you can read the menu on the Diner wall, you could look to words as a duchess looks to jewels. You are hungry. You want food and drink that you can have.

You will probably not notice Aaron Elroy as he steps out the back door to clean the patio and wipe your table. If you do notice him you will think *cute boy* or *pecker-headed motherfucker* or *honkie* or *good to see working youth*. His hat makes him look younger than he already looks, but you will never see Aaron Elroy without it. You may want to if you are the loping tall man always in the white suit. Then you will call him in the middle of his shift and describe yourself via your height and love to meet him after work. Otherwise you will probably not see Aaron Elroy. But you may nonetheless lift your feet while he slides the mop in the vicinity of your stool.

As you dine in late evening you might hear the sizzle-pop of insects frying themselves on the hot blue light on the south side of the patio. If you do hear these brief bursts of death, you will not know that the blue light near the patio ceiling is the reason Aaron Elroy wears the Doggie Diner uniform. His father created the lamp and the Diner company ordered two dozen to install in their open-air stores. Bugs get zapped; boy gets a summer job.

The blue light has been father Elroy's most demanding invention, not on account of technical or manufacturing complications, but for the same reason the men at Los Alamos had trouble putting the atomic bomb on the market. Inventing destruction is not without cumber.

Before putting the *Blue BugBarian* on paper, Elroy spent the good part of two weeks observing and comparing other readily available forms of killing. He went to the Orinda Hardware store and bought a mouse trap, mosquito spray, ant poison, snail killer, adhesive fly catcher strip, rat poison, and a new earwig exterminator. As he scanned the store's arsenal, he noticed that en règle générale life's smaller creatures tend to be the least wanted. In any case, they are the cheapest to eliminate. A community of ants can be done in for a dollar fifty-nine. For thirty-nine cents your kitchen flies can be kissed goodbye. A single box of Bagetta – marked down from one twenty-nine to under a dollar – will get all the snails in your garden. Rats are the biggest thing you can kill for under three dollars. But, Elroy noted, there was nothing on sale to eliminate cats, llamas, rabbits, cows, beavers and the like. For these you have to go to the gun shop or buy an expensive metal trap.

Father Elroy spent the first day of June in his rose patch watching snails eat their last meal. As he lay in the woodchips catching intermittent whiffs of his scarlet wide-bloomed President Eisenhowers, he observed a family (he thought) of gastropods head for lunch. Each left a shiny trail that ended at a Bagetta pellet. The creatures nibbled through the first game of a Giant-Pirate doubleheader (Elroy had it piping out of the window of his son's bedroom), then withdrew into their shells to expire. Was the execution ethical? Would not the *Blue BugBarian* kill more mercifully? *Yes* (he thought): *better to die of an instantaneous shock than to succumb to Eternal Darkness (maybe) at the dinner table. But* (he asked himself as Marichal was high kicking down the Pirates in the second game) *was it really necessary to kill garden snails in order to preserve the roses? Maybe not.* At six zip in the bottom of the fifth (Mays was two for two with a walk and a stolen base) he envisioned an invention that would save the flowers and not only spare the gastropods, but actually give them a better life. He foresaw in a corner of the garden a sort of miniature Disneyland that would attract the creatures through a tiny MAIN GATE. They would be channelled down MAIN STREET to a series of loops, holes, mazes, and snail-size mountains which would entertain them and make them forget any and all intention of rose eating. The vision was clear but would be costly, and Elroy feared America was not ready to pay the necessary price for SNAILEY-LAND when a ninety-nine-cent box of Bagetta would do. He did (he thought) understand the limits of human compassion. Man (he knew) always draws the line somewhere. Bald eagles, *yes*. Snails and slugs, *no*.

Convinced that his *Blue BugBarian* would be a kinder killer than poison pellets, Elroy spent the next day observing the slaughter of termites. He rode around in a green and black minivan with a pleasant ponytailed employee from Jensen's TNT (Terminate Noxious Termites). He watched the young man douse community after community with his miracle canister. The insects, once showered, had a few seconds to squirm and kick their legs before rolling on their backs to die. Elroy estimated that from eight am to five pm, excluding an hour for lunch, the young man killed between seven and ten thousand termites. He figured about 250 bugs per square foot and about 35 square feet of dousing. The higher estimate took into account soldier termites that might have been out of the area at spray time, but which (according to Jensen's man) would probably bite the dust when they got home.

As Elroy drove back to Orinda that evening he pondered thus: *the* Blue BugBarian *is selective; it kills only flying insects and only those that happen to fly into it (true, the blue light attracts); you go to it – it doesn't come to you. Other advantages included: no massive indiscriminate murder, instantaneous expiration, and no unsavory smell for nearby eaters.* The only disavantage he could think of was death.

For dinner his wife had prepared mint lamb chops, tossed salad, gratin potatoes, and lemon custard. With dessert Elroy laid out what he saw to be the beauties of his invention in juxtaposition with what he had witnessed that day. His wife was able to digest the image of the blue light with her custard but asked her husband to leave the writhing pale bodies of the *Kalotermitidae* family until after the meal.

Before finally giving the manufacturer the green light on the *Blue BugBarian*, Elroy had caught three mice, poisoned a rat, had seen flies die of exhaustion on yellow adhesive paper, and had sprayed societies of earwigs and mosquitoes. He also went to the chicken farm east of Livermore for an afternoon of fowl beheading.

He ultimately reasoned in favour of bringing the *Blue BugBarian* into being as follows:

1. death is inevitable
2. it's no fun
3. better you go to it than it come to you
4. make it quick
5. we should make the world a better place to live in
6. and die in
7. flying insects don't mix with outdoor eating
8. best to zap them

He tried to fit the Golden Rule somewhere into his *logica absolutus*, but he was aware (he thought) of the pitfalls of anthropomorphism.

*

Neil Baker's foot lay on the pedal pushing up twenty-four toward the Caldecott Tunnel. He twisted a Salem out of his shirt pocket, lit it and sucked deeply. The smoke didn't quite meet the gut pain but he felt some kind of interaction. A minor distaste turned instantly to a soothing, like a dive in a cool lake.

On the other side of the tunnel, he let the Falcon sedan go plunging at eighty toward Orinda. It rattled until it met the upgrade before Lafayette slowing to fifty. He turned off Newell Avenue, the first Walnut Creek exit, then right on Clay Road to home. He pulled into the gravel semi-circle in front of the house; the headlights blackened on Billy's curtains. He lit another Salem before opening the front door.

His wife wasn't on the couch with MuMu, Bunny's shaggy stuffed alligator. He followed the kitchen light to the patio where the cockchafer larva lay on a birch leaf in a powdered glow. He pulled a thin branch from the tree and prodded the shiny mass near the legs. Legs wiggled and the stubby-pickle toes curled inward then opened slowly to full length. He ran the stick from the navel up the body to the nape and poked ever so gently. The cockchafer twitched twice before returning to rest. He walked around the leaf to let light fall on the eyes and sleeping lips. He prodded the lower lip with the point of the branch, then cast the stick aside and went off towards bed.

I said in my heart concerning the sons of men, that God would prove them, and show them to be like beasts. Therefore the death of one man, and of beasts is one, and the condition of them both is equal. As man dieth, so they also die. All things breath alike, and man hath nothing more than beast. All things are subject to vanity. And all things go to one place: of earth they were made, and into earth they return together. Who knoweth if the spirit of the children of Adam ascend upward, and if the spirit of beasts descend downward? And I have found that nothing is better than for a man to rejoice in his work, and that this is his portion. For who shall bring him to know the things that shall be after him?

Ecclesiastes 3

"Get your ass in here, kid. Looks like we got an early bar rush." Aaron wheeled the mop bucket to the toilet door and hurried into the cage.

"Take the grill, kid. I got the windows. You got a pair a big cheese no mo and four, one's out."

"What's the other big?"

"That's a Western all the way."

Baker made a pair of Big Chili Dogs and dropped them on the counter at window 4.

"Hey man, can you put the shit in a bag. Wha you think – that I'm eaten bofa'em here?"

"Drinkin summin?" Baker asked hurriedly. There were now five customers at the windows.

"Yeah. Gimme a chocolate shake and a big Coke?"

"Neil, pick up a pair a big cheese no mo. These four… are they walkin'?"

"Hell if I know. Yeah, walk em," Baker said as he squirted chocolate syrup into the bottom of a twelve-ounce cup. He glanced to the corner window and said, "Help ya ma'am?"

"Yezz… I'd like three large chili dogs with very, very few onions on them, and three orders of fries, and three small orange drinks." The voice was high pitched and sweet and the neck rotated between clauses. Baker's eyes fell on the bare brown chest, V-ed by nectarine silk. He held the shake under the mixer blade and looked into the V… six or seven looping black hairs pasted to the sternum. The neck rotated. The eyes didn't flinch. "And if you might put all that in a bag please," the voice said with upper-octaval sweetness. Baker's mouth twisted and the lines in his forehead deepened because Neil Baker had *never called a muthafuckin man a woman before*, so he shouted to Aaron, "take care a this guy at window six!" Then capping the shake that went with the two big chili dogs he mumbled: "Ah be gawdammed if I'm gunna call a man a woman."

Aaron pulled the four burgers off the grill and bagged them leaving the one without onions on the right. "Pick up four Neil, one's out on your right." Then he turned to window 6, "Excuse me Ma'am, what was your order again?"

The voice repeated with the same honeyed tone.

"I got a Western all the way," he called to Baker while dropping three handfuls of fries into the mesh basket and plunging them into the grease.

"Gimme a pair, one's no red, the other's cheese."

"And I need three big chili dogs light O and three small oranges." He asked the woman if it was to go.

"Walk it all, Neil." he said.

"Later Jack!" the guy at window 4 said. When he turned up the sidewalk Baker saw a good foot and a bent foot that swung at the end of the tibia. The man wore flip-flops. One foot flip-flopped, the other didn't.

"Pick up three big chili dogs for some ass rammin!" Baker piped.

The voice at window 6 said, "I thank you kindly young man," when Aaron hoisted two Doggie Diner bags to the counter. Their face was like chestnut wax on a picket, rotating, which it did while leaving the

Diner, then again, three or four times, as it crossed East 14th in the middle of the block.

Friday, June 24, 1957. Ernie Felton, Pete Culperston, Tony Tobbs, and Mrs. Iris Casterhaven sat behind the wheels of their empty school buses, the four lined up like railway cars. Turk McPheeter, twenty-seven years a handyman with the Foothill School system, filled tank after tank from the school pump. When Iris Casterhaven pulled out he called, "Don't run 'er inta the bay Walrus." Iris tapped the side of her machine with her open left hand and called back, "The kids ain't huntin' no fish tonight."

The two hundred forty-two members of the Las Lomas senior class climbed rather quietly in their tuxes and long dresses into the yellow buses. Iris Casterhaven's was the last to fill up and Neil Baker was the last one in at the school parking lot. He had spent the afternoon in the backyard trying to get a facial suntan in hopes that it might help. In four years of high school he hadn't had even as much as a thigh. After half an hour in the sun he fell asleep on a striped beach towel, his head falling to the left. He awoke two hours later, at almost five, in the shade of a long-needled conifer, the right side of his face a steamed tomato. He hurried into the house and into his baby-blue tux from Smith's Rentals. The sash affair around the waist cost him a couple of minutes but he was on the bus before Iris Casterhaven had her out of the parking lot at a quarter to six.

There were half a dozen free seats on the bus when Neil poked the pale side of his face past the three steps toward the congregation of angels waiting to flutter into the Senior All Night. When the busload got a look at Neil's full face the chairs squeaked, the girls snickered, and the boys on the football team gave him the works.

"Hey Neil Baby, looks like Mommy forgot to take you out of the oven."

"Well get a load a Pocahontas's half-brother, will ya?"

"Bake a Baker… just add milk."

"Halloween was six months ago, Baker Boy."

"We'll chuck ya in the bay to put out the fire."

The girls howled now, even Cindy Talbot, until Iris finally went heavy on the horn and said if they kept this crap up they'd never get out of Walnut Creek.

Baker slid into the first available seat. He looked straight ahead trying to freeze his tear ducts. The bus calmed until Wally Webster, the defensive captain, shouted, "What's for dinner, folks…? Barbecued Baker?" The racket started again and what Baker knew would happen happened. Beneath the silk black sash, the gut pain was lodging. Cindy Talbot looked at the boy next to her. She stopped laughing. The sunburnt side of his face was outlined by a fresh crew cut. His right eyelid seemed to bulge and the eyebrow cut a ridge at the base of the forehead. Without thinking she put her hand on Baker's knee.

She said, "Hey, don't you worry about it," in a voice as soft as her hand.

Iris had them past the Caldecott Tunnel heading for the toll gate of the Bay Bridge. The hand was gone, but so was hurt.

As the bus hurtled up the first mile of the bridge, Baker found the courage to look at the girl by his side. She was in a pine green dress that had colourful circles and rectangles haphazardly arranged, sometimes overlapping, sometimes not. She had a string of pearls about her narrow neck and three miniature pearls dangling from gold chains below each ear. Her cheeks were powdered pink and what Baker could see of her eyes was grey. Her hair was the page boy cut of the times, and Cindy Talbot smelled like the ladies' toiletry aisle in Woolworth's. Baker's senses were simultaneously attuned to femininity. He felt like licking the neck muscle that reached into her jaw.

Instead he shivered like a bird with a broken wing.

The four buses arrived at Fisherman's Wharf at 19:35. The passengers filed from bus to boat carrying hundreds of hurly-burly hopes, hidden flasks of hard stuff, and a few human prayers. They would cruise the bay until three-thirty in the morning. Wally Webster would see Neil Baker only once that night and be too drunk to notice him. Wally Webster would corner Debbie Clayton in the girl's lavatory shortly after midnight. He would feel her up and shoot half a wad into his silk sash. He would live to lie about it. Neil Baker would spend most of the evening staring affectionately at the bay fog from the starboard railing. He would finally talk with Cindy Talbot on Iris's bus on the way home. He would walk her home and hold her tightly next to the Talbot mailbox in the half-light of dawn. She would reciprocate, as far as he could understand. He wouldn't kiss her because he wouldn't dare. He would hold her tightly, and he would feel the muscles round his eyes gather and pinch at the top of his nose bone.

Iris Casterhaven would fall into bed at six fifteen knowing that she wouldn't work again until September.

She and Neil Baker would squeeze half their pillows while they worked their way into a deep corner of heaven's terrestrial hold.

*

Friday, July 22, 1957. Cindy and Neil were wed in the Walnut Creek Presbyterian Church at three o'clock sharp. Only the lonely know how four weeks can suffice to put strangers in a nuptial bed.

They rode in Neil's father's Buick to the Holiday Inn in Concord. Cindy, now Cyndy, stroked the flesh around her husband's right femur. His suit pants were lowered to his knees hanging loosely near the emergency brake knob. She said she didn't know if she could wait til they got to the motel room and that she hadn't known what love was til now. As he drove, she grabbed his head with both hands and sniffed it as if it were a melon. Then she dug her tongue into his ear. This – tongue in ear – she had been saving for the day of marriage, but its effect was other than what was intended. Though Baker didn't conceive it as such, it was as if his union with wife was a rubber raft and the first drift of air had just slipped through a tiny leak. Eventually the raft would flatten leaving it a useless toy for two growing children. The tongue in the ear was a minor puncture, soon forgotten, but nonetheless an irritation.

Baker aimed the Buick toward the Concord exit.

Mr. and Mrs. Neil Baker were escorted to their honeymoon suite, Room 217 overlooking the pool, by a thin man who used to be a caddie at the Orinda Country Club. For nine years Charlie Dunn took the bus from Richmond to the Orinda station which was a mile from the golf course. He would walk up El Sobrante under the oak trees, past the four- and five-bedroom houses to the clubhouse, then carry double bags over eighteen fairways. He had been the favourite of Dr. and Mrs. Wainwright because he never said more than "da flag is at da back" or "Thank ya kinely, ma'am," when Dr. Wainwright handed him eleven dollars behind the eighteenth green. After nine years of toting double bags, Charlie Dunn's lower back provoked a gaunt facial grimace and a question from Dr. Wainwright, "Are you okay, Charlie?" "Mah back dun hurt, doc," Charlie had said deferentially. The doctor kneaded his caddie's back with the grip end of his putter, then told him that maybe he should change professions. That same day the Wainwrights gave Charlie fifteen dollars and shook his hand and never saw him again.

He opened room 217, placed the suitcase at the foot of the bed, and said "thank ya kinely, sir" when Neil Baker slid two quarters into his palm.

Wedding dresses have never been made in a slip-on slip-off fashion. Baker fought with a dozen buttons on his wife's spine before releasing the first layer of clothing. She dove to the bed, her arms extended like an Olympic swimmer off the start pedestal. She turned onto her back and took a position where her torso and legs resembled the wishbone of a chicken. She began wiggling out of her girdle, but Baker stopped her. He wanted to undress her – the way he had undressed a thousand women in English class, in Sunday School, in front of television, in his mother's magazines, and in the darkness under his ruffled bedspread. And he wanted to watch himself do it.

"Honey, my belly's gunna blow up in yur face, 'f ya don't shake a leg!" Cyndy exclaimed between heartbeats.

Neil said nothing and saw himself unsnap the garter buttons and pull the hose off the narrow white thighs. Then he wedged his fingers between the hips and girdle and worked the thing toward the knees. As he did so he saw himself seeing silky embroidered underpants that began to fall with the girdle. He dropped these too to the knees. Cyndy sensed he was doing what he had always wanted to do. She kept quiet, letting alone the gentle shuffle of fabric and the sound of skin. She closed her eyes.

Pulling all his wife's lower underclothes past her feet, Neil Baker dropped to one knee beside the bed.

The thousand women he had stripped before had always sent sparks to his groin and blood to the fire hose. This one, the first one at his fingertips, did nothing of the sort. He was as calm as a veterinary surgeon as he stared at the joint of the wishbone. He wondered – in his own way – if sedation was a by-product of love, like when a cat lethargically drops a dead mouse from its mouth.

He stood up and hoisted Cyndy to a sitting position. He moved behind her and easily unlatched her brassiere. It fell free of her arms and she dropped back onto the bed. Neil looked at her wanting to take off something else – maybe the skin or hair, the bush, or the toenails. But there was nothing more to remove. This was nakedness.

Eventually, Baker was able to put his wife into the pocket of his head where the thousand other women lay clanging. Then he was able to screw her and she him.

It was their wedding night.

*

dzzt

Dzzt

dz   dZZZZ

> *dzt   dzzz*

dzz   dzzt   Dz   Dzzt

DZZ   dz   dzzz

dzt

Dzz   dzDzz   dzt
dzt

As he mopped the empty Doggie Diner patio, Aaron Elroy counted eighteen BLUE BUGBARIAN victims in forty-five seconds. Figuring about seventy (plus a few) forty-five seconds per hour times eighteen, that made over a thousand victims an hour. The Diner was a twenty-four-hour operation. Summer nights were roughly from nine to four in the morning. Seven times a thousand, 7,000 a day. And that was at the hand of just one ten-inch blue light.

When Aaron had turned twelve his church had given him the honour of the Priesthood. He, in turn, had honoured his church by memorising the first chapter of Genesis. After calculating the bug deaths in the Diner that evening, he recalled that God had said: *Let the waters ring forth the creeping creature having life, and the fowl that may fly over the earth under the firmament of heaven.*

Was the Doggie Diner patio "the firmament of heaven"?

And God saw all the things that he had made, and they were good.

Was he crazy to think that insects were "fowl"? Were they? Or did they fit in with "creeping creature"? There was no mention of insects as far as he could remember. Didn't they count? But *good were all the things that He had made.* Maybe He didn't make mosquitos. Maybe they grew later out of swamps. Did He make swamps?

Aaron finished the patio and got ready for his twenty-minute break. It was quarter to midnight and so quiet you could hear the hum from the Coke machine. Aaron cooked himself a Big Cheese Burger and concocted a root beer freeze, though it wasn't on the menu. He took off his hat and apron and went to a stool in the patio.

dzzz

dz

Dzzt

A shiny missile-like white convertible pulled into the parking lot. From the throne on the driver's side exited the six-foot-five man in the white suit. His walk was loping, hands slightly away from the hips and turned to the outside, eyes bouncing in slow cushioned rhythm with the cream leather shoes which landed toe first. He spotted Aaron eating and installed himself, legs crossed just above the knee, on the stool across the table. Aaron felt an immediate shortness of breath, like when he had to address the congregation at Sunday School.

"I wuzz juz in the neighbahood and thought I might juz have a light burger. How you been doin?"

(Our Father in heaven, please help me so that no bodily harm might come from this and that this man might find his own happiness elsewhere.)

"I'm working a lot, you know, trying to pay for my school."

"Yez, I thought you looked lak a univerzity type person, juz from the way you show politenezz to the cuztomerz. And where might you be purzooing studeez?"

"Uh, I go to BYU in Utah."

"Yez, Utah. Now thaz somewhere in Wyaming, izn't it?"

"Well, it's near it."

"Yez, I see. And I imagine that you are in the field of mathamatics."

"Well, I don't really know what I'm going into."

"The mathamatics wuz my bezt subject when I wuz in school."

"Where did you go?"

"That wuz when I wuz at Castlemont High. And I enjoyed hiztory – yez – in addition."

When he had called Aaron at the Diner, the man in the white suit had had a mellifluous pant in his voice. Aaron had been afraid. Across the table, the man made Aaron feel like he was a Christian. He was making peace with a wayward angel, but he felt part of himself disappear as the angel's floating dog-brown eyes worked their way under his clothes. Then he thought:

And God saw all the things that he had made, and they were good.

And then the angel said: "How bout you and me hookin up when you get off, juz for a drink?"

As the shivers hit, Neil Baker put his head out of window 6 and said: "Why don't you leave the sonabitch alone you muthafucka?"

And with that the angel flew in shiny white missile into the middle of the night.

*

When Cyndy Baker awoke on the couch the next morning, her husband was dead. The phone rang at seven and after the seventh ring she screamed, *"Neil! Answer the gaddam phone!"* At the twelfth ring she picked it up and slammed it down in one motion. Five minutes later when it sounded again, she answered thinking it might be Neil. The policeman identified her, then himself, then said Mr. Baker had driven into the wall at the entrance to the Caldecott Tunnel and had expired in an envelope of flames. It had taken three hours to find out who he was.

Cyndy headed for the sour mash leaving the receiver on the floor. She lamented in the pattern death is usually lamented: the other, the self, the condition of life in general, then a return to the self or the other. In her case she finished with grief of the self, concurrent with the pouring of the last swig from the bottle of Old Crow.

Neil Baker did and did not commit suicide. He did steer the Falcon toward the wall with a certain noetic conviction. He knew change would be brought about. But Baker, like all killers of self, did not know what death would bring. Change, yes. But what change? As he approached the tunnel wall his thinking, though steamed, had a germ of "now what?" that left his death open-ended. In this sense "suicide" is the wrong word.

After the policeman's phone call Cyndy Baker spent the remainder of the day in the triangle marked off by the couch, the matrimonial bed, and the chaise longue on the back patio. Around noon she called her mother in Walnut Creek. Mrs. Talbot came to find her daughter in a puddle of beer on the couch and Bunny and Billy Nabisco flooding the back lawn with sprinklers and garden hoses. Cyndy repeatedly asked her mother, *What the hell am I going to do now?* knowing full well that she'd do what she had been doing, minus Neil.

Mrs. Talbot told her that Neil had been a good husband because *not many men got off work at two in the morning and got up with the kids at seven.* Cyndy said yes, she knew, and asked her mother to go to the store for drink.

*

Elroy sits in church on the green bench behind the fourth tee at Tilden. He looks heavenward at this downhill par four, three hundred sixty yards. He folds His arms, leans back, extends His legs. He inhales the

138

given air that is cooled by the evening fog bank rolling close to the treetops. No one is playing the third hole, so He sits.

I am fading my driver but when I hit it right nothing is better. I could play a three-iron and keep it in the fairway. I could play two balls.

The fairway is narrow off the tee, widens for anything hit two hundred yards, then narrows to the kidney green. It is tree-lined all the way.

He doesn't play golf with a watch. Some gifts are boundless. The sun is gone. He unzips the side pocket of His bag and removes His navy-blue alpaca sweater. He looks up into the fog. Angel hair.

I love my driver though it often does me wrong. It says MacGregor. For me it is MacElroy. I forgive it as I forgive myself. It and I will now hit.

The shot starts clean but as it rises it fades. It tumbles on the right edge of the fairway and stops short of the trees in the light rough. He picks up His bag and follows the ball.

Death has discovered my son
Eyes wide he tries to run.
Baker's boom, Baker's tomb
Aaron's first lick of doom.
To the floor he rubs his knees
God I hope I'm not in the trees.

Bless all that is, will be and has been
Pray that I have a shot at the pin.

He does and makes par. He bogeys five, six, and seven. At eight, a twenty-footer sneaks into the left side of the cup. Birdie. A par at nine will give Him a forty-one on the front.

He chases his drive into the woods.

Find it or not but be of good cheer
The clubhouse is never out of beer.

It loses Him. He walks in not bothering to play another ball. The Kingdom is without numbers, He thinks. Beer, and He flies homeward. Heaven expands.

*

Though her mother told her it made little sense, Cyndy Baker insisted on a lavish funeral. The Mossbauer people from Mossbauer's Mortuary in Pleasant Hill were happy to make it lavish. Cyndy was told that her husband would probably be best served in a copper-plated coffin with zinc lining and a bed of

Norwegian goose feathers covered with China's finest salmon-coloured silk. The box cost less than a new automobile and since Baker wouldn't be driving any more, his wife said that would be fine.

There would be no viewing of the body because there wasn't enough of it left to make Baker recognisable except possibly to Cyndy, and even that was questionable. However, the Mossbauers arranged for an evening around the coffin for family and close friends. For this ten dozen chrysanthemums were ordered from Felix Mossbauer's cousin who had a floral shop across the street.

The funeral was held the next day with an additional ten dozen flowers. Cyndy said there were ten commandments so there should be ten dozen flowers. This time she insisted on yellow roses. Aaron was the only person to attend the funeral who had not been around the coffin the night before. At the end of the ceremony he helped carry his friend to the hearse with the assistance of Cyndy's brother Merle, Baker's Uncle Eamon from Fresno, and Felix Mossbauer. As they slid the coffin into the car, Aaron bit a hole in his lower lip.

When the procession drove into the cemetery at the west end of Concord, there were four cars instead of the original five. Uncle Eamon had been last and had needed to stop for gas. He pulled off the freeway at the last Pleasant Hill exit, filled up, and decided that by the time he found the place it'd all be over with anyway. He drove straight back to Fresno.

Aaron was now last, alone in his father's Cadillac. As he parked the car holding a handkerchief to his bloody lower lip, for the first time in his twenty years of life, God and His Universe of Goodness felt loose.

The coffin was lowered into the earth at 11:45. The only long stream of tears was on Aaron Elroy's face.

No plans had been made for after the burial. Uncle Eamon was gone and Baker's parents were dead, so Mrs. Talbot took it upon herself to lead the group from the cemetery. She suggested they go to The Hickory Pit for what she called the best barbecued ribs in Contra Costa County. Cyndy said she'd rather go to Frasier's Ice Cream Parlor, but first she'd have to pick up the kids cause the sitter could only stay til one. Mrs. Talbot agreed to Frasier's because it was Cyndy's husband who had died and not her own.

They were ten plus Bunny and Billy Nabisco when they settled into Frasier's largest booth and picked up the colourful plastic-coated menus, their eyes sinking in unison to the pictures and prices.

*

Aaron worked three more weeks at the Diner before going back to school. Neil Baker was replaced by Kenny Erdman. He gave Aaron few orders, did some of the dirty work himself, and had a habit of ringing up 0.00 on the register when a three-dollar order was paid. Mysteriously, the shift averaged twenty dollars less a night after Baker's death. On their last night together Aaron asked Kenny Erdman why he lifted from the till and if he didn't think it was wrong to rob the people who pay your salary. Kenny Erdman said he was divorced and had two kids and this was the only way he could keep food in everybody's mouth. He said this as if he were sharing a great secret. In fact he had no children but sometimes wished he did.

Of the two thousand dollars Aaron made that summer, eight hundred went to buy his first car. He laid eight one-hundred-dollar bills face up on the manager's desk at the OK CAR-RAL on East 14th, and in so doing felt himself inch into manhood. A butterfly crawling through the cocoon. He drove away in a beige beetle, Volkswagen genus.

Two days later Aaron packed his duffel bag and left a tearful mother and waving father at the foot of the driveway. "Enjoy yourself, son. These last two might be the best years of your life," his father had said. "I love you son" had been his mother's choked parting words.

Aaron fought tears himself until the beetle scurried in amid the afternoon traffic on Highway 24 East. Then he felt himself "away", a twenty-year-old at the controls of his own wheels. Fifteen hours to Provo, but he'd take a day and a half.

Aaron would go where his father hadn't been. Into Harlot's Web he'd fly. Elroy had dallied under the formica table of the Hot Shoppe in New York until his wing was too soggy to flutter. Aaron, however, saw all things that He had made and they were good, and the boys in high school had told him of the very good things a few miles outside of Reno.

Plus or minus a few cognitive jolts, Aaron reasoned thus his trip to Moonlight Ranch:

1. all things He had made were good
2. He was becoming a question mark
3. he had held out til twenty which wasn't bad considering the universal average
4. though it might be illegal in Zion, it was legal in Nevada
5. it was definitely illegal at BYU and he'd be spending the next eight months there
6. he had no girlfriend so he wouldn't be cheating on anybody
7. his father would probably approve

8. his mother would probably never find out
    since the odds were he'd get out of the
    place alive

In fact, Aaron's logic was but a grain of sand trying to make sense of a tidal wave. *Let the waters that are under the heaven be gathered together into one place.* That one place was atop the middle of the driver's seat in the beige Volkswagen putt-putting through the mountain pines toward Reno.

*

The only witness Martha Elroy and Ray Hiller had had when they stood in the chamber of the Justice of the Peace was the same yellow moon that was to hang outside the Hotel Otter the night Martha and Mandy slept there.

They got to Reno at three in the morning and made straight for Judge Burt Prudhomme's house. The Judge answered the door in bathrobe and slippers and agreed to perform the ceremony only when Martha said, "Your Honoured, it's now or for never." Mrs. Prudhomme served as the legal witness though she slept soundly through all the promises.

When the newlyweds got back in their '34 Studebaker Ray said, "By the light of the moon, Martha, I thee wed." There it was bobbing outside their windshield big as a pancake as they headed east on Route 40 past Sparks, bound for middle of the Nevada desert.

"Getting married," Ray said, "is between you and me and that yaller moon." Martha rubbed her chestnut hair into Ray's neck. "You and me gunna drive out there till we don't see nobody but the sagebrush, then we gunna lay us down in the middle of nuthin, then nuthin's gunna be evrathin." Martha's chestnut hair fell into Ray's lap.

Behind them the sun poked up like half a flower on the rim of the Sierra Nevada. The eyes of the Studebaker lost their glow to the purple lines in the synclines that rose in front of them. Ray dropped his right hand from the steering wheel and twisted his fingers in Martha's curls and scrape-gripped her scalp.

The powdery light on the desert ridges hardened to baby blue. Route 40 opened wide as the Studebaker spun toward Lovelock.

*

Aaron stood in front of the cast-iron gate under a canopy of stars and a conical lamp. The ground was soft and dusty. He rang the bell; the gate clicked open. His gut led His head forward to the main trailer door which in turn clicked open. Before Him a rainbow of chiffon cloaked a semi-circular coterie of freshly bathed angels. Debbora, Diana, Docras, Dina, Jairus, Jezabel, Joanna, Judith, Sara, Sarai, Sephora, and Elizabeth. There was a bar on the right.

Aaron's eyes were exceedingly glazed. He was unable to distinguish faces; he saw only the celestial rainbow. When He took three steps toward the bar, the colours separated. Jezabel was big-breasted lime green. She drifted directly to Aaron. She took His hand and led Him eastward for twenty minutes of Lies. The shores were dry and though it was quick, she said He was hurting her.

When He returned, He went to the bar to sit and look. This time Elizabeth did not hesitate and floated to His side without touching Him. She saw in Aaron's face and on His watch that He had lived Lies. "Jezabel is a bitch," she whispered.

They talked without touching over beer while other men came and went. She was a student at San Francisco State; she did not love her boyfriend; she gave Him her phone number for when He'd be home at Christmas. He, she now knew, was and was not

Mormon and had a face of love.

She led Him through a corridor to the northern trailer for two and a half hours of Truth.

*

Elroy is back on the golf course. His drive at nine has faded far to the right. He picks up his bag and heads off, this time intent on finding his ball.

The ninth fairway, he presumes, is somewhere between the Big and Little Dippers – the only asterisms of which he knows the names. The course has been designed with respect for the indigenous terrain, there being no planes or surfaces except for one aged eucalyptus tree. Elroy thinks his ball is behind the tree. He is walking toward it on less than water. The tree looks close but it is far.

He walks and walks. The tree does not get bigger.

Here the light is like late October at five in the afternoon. Pulchritudinous. His favourite time of the year.

He keeps walking. There is nothing before him except the tree, so his ball, he thinks, must be behind it. But the tree does not get bigger. It floats in its sameness in a fine October mist.

Elroy thinks he walks for twenty years. Thirty years. Forty-five years. Now, finally, the tree gets bigger. He will reach it. The walking and waiting have made him wary. He approaches the eucalyptus with apprehension and small steps. He is now before it. He lays a hand on the bark. It feels funny, unlike his hands on other trees. Then, timorously, he peeps round the tree. The ball is there, its silver-white lustre peeping back at him through the October afternoon mist. Elroy waxes blissful.

He looks off down the fairway. Seeing nothingness, he looks back at his ball and removes a seven iron from his bag. He loops the club behind his shoulders and notices that the branches overhead will not inhibit his swing. He then sets himself over the ball wiggling his hips and adjusting his fingers on the grip. He is settled, ready to hit. He stares at the ball fixedly. Then: slowly, very slowly, the ball begins to dim and lose its sheen. Elroy realizes that his own light is dimming at the same slow steady pace. He looks up at the tree and down at his golf bag and they are likewise greying. Then everything – ball, tree, bag and seven iron – fade into the October light. Elroy is the candle that is flickering out at the end of its wick.

At the moment of blackening Elroy feels the seven-iron slip from his hands.

"*Holy Jesus!*" he screams, his head flying from the bed, his hands reaching his limp pecker, his wife groping for the light.

*

That morning Joan was up early getting started on the applesauce raisin cake and pot roast before church. After breakfast Elroy went out to mow the lawn and trim the pyracantha. While he was mowing he foresaw the possibility of a mower with an extra set of blades on either side of the machine that could fold down and clamp into cutting position when one was attacking the open stretches of grass. *The machine has promise*, Elroy thought, *as long as it takes up little additional space in the crowded American shed.* Before he finished the lawn, Joan came out to ask him if he planned on going to church with her. "Sure, honey," he said, and killed the engine.

Sister Sprewer the Sunday School teacher gave a lesson on holding to the rod and sticking to the straight and narrow path in these latter days. She said there were *false prophets among us who were trying to bend the rod and get us to stray off the Lord's highway.* When she said these things *in the name of*

Jesus Christ amen, Elroy thought of his dream and winced.

After church they went to Concord to get Martha. Though weekends were bad for TV, they found her in her orange chair in front of the set. "We thought you might want to come over for Elroy's birthday?" Joan said. "Rilda's coming, and Wayne said he might be down from Tahoe." Martha said she had nothing better to do.

They drove to Orinda between autumnal hills.

"Damn pretty sometimes," Martha said.

Joan laid the table putting the cake with all forty-five candles in the middle of a halo of the season's last scarlet President Eisenhowers. She set two more places when the Seamans unexpectedly showed up with a present. They said they'd be delighted to stay for dinner.

When they had all assembled round the table, Bob Seaman asked Elroy to open the gift. It was a six-pack of imported German brew. Seaman drew an opener from his shirt pocket and uncapped a bottle for Elroy and one for himself. His proposed toast to the birthday boy was delayed, at Joan's gentle request, till after the food had been rightly blessed.

Find out more about Jon Ferguson
and his works at his author website:
www.jonfergusonbooks.com,
where you can also sign up for updates.

Please contribute an honest online review;
it's the easiest and most supportive thing a reader can do
for an author and/or a small independent press.
editor@hugejam.com